D0434891

Tantalize

Tantalize

Cynthia Leitich Smith

CANDLEWICK PRESS
CAMBRIDGE, MASSACHUSETTS

Copyright © 2007 by Cynthia Leitich Smith

First edition 2007

Library of Congress Cataloging-in-Publication Data

Smith, Cynthia Leitich.
Tantalize / Cynthia Leitich Smith. — 1st ed.
p.   cm.
Summary: When multiple murders in Austin, Texas, threaten the grand
re-opening of her family's vampire-themed restaurant, seventeen-year-old,
orphaned Quincie worries that her best friend-turned-love interest,
Keiren, a werewolf-in-training, may be the prime suspect.
ISBN 978-0-7636-2791-1
[1. Supernatural—Fiction. 2. Restaurants—Fiction. 3. Vampires—Fiction.
4. Werewolves—Fiction. 5. Orphans—Fiction. 6. Austin (Tex.)—Fiction.]
I. Title.
PZ7.S64464Tan 2007
[Fic]—dc22   2005058124

6 8 10 9 7 5

Printed in the United States of America

This book was typeset in Galliard.

Candlewick Press
2067 Massachusetts Avenue
Cambridge, Massachusetts 02140

visit us at www.candlewick.com

For Greg

"I never drink . . . wine."

—BELA LUGOSI'S DRACULA

CONTENTS

❧ *antipasto* ❧

Innocenza	3
Fangs Are Us	7
Man or Wolf-Man, the Boy Was Mine	13
Questioning	19
Every Dog Has His Day	26
Blood Relations	31
Blood Pressure	35
The Facts of Life	40
Twice Shy	47
Watch Dog	54
The Scene of the Crime	60
I Vant to Suck Your Blood	66

❧ *primo* ❧

From Blah to Bite	73
The Monster Maker	83
School and Other Sucky Things	91
Fang Shui	98

All the World's a Stage   106

Moon Lite   112

Home Work   124

Metamorphoses   130

No Rest for the Wicked   135

Faith   140

Mystery   143

Poof!   149

Playing Dead   153

Playing Dumb   159

Bat Man   163

Prey or Predator   167

Everybody's Got a Dark Side   174

✤ *secondo* ✤

Forever Young   181

Brad the Impaler   186

Carpe Noctem   193

The Prince of Transylvania   198

"I Could Have Danced All Night"   204

Little Freddie Munster   210

"In a Glass Darkly"   214

Tipsy   220

The Morning After   222

My Own Free Vill   228

Sheep's Clothing   233

Dragons and Dungeons   237

Pillow Talk   244

⚞ dolce ⚟

Baby Got Bite   251

Dental Care   258

Angel MIA   261

Dead Woman Running   266

"Nightwing"   270

High Protein, Low Carb   275

Cat and Louse   280

The Silver Bullet   284

Hearts at Stake   290

This Side of Heaven   296

A Drinking Problem   301

This Side of Hell   304

⚞ contorno ⚟

Author's Note   314

Acknowledgments   317

antipasto

like the inside of a conch shell. So, I imagined picking one up, a curved shell, and shaking it to see if the animal within had died.

Then Kieren's fingernails began tracing the pattern on my upturned palm, and it was hard to think about anything. I knew it bothered him, though, my laugh line, my love line, my lifeline. Slight and severed, all of them.

This was four years ago, so we were in middle school, past due for handholding. I'd been staying with Kieren's family, helping with the baby, while my folks were in Guatemala doing whatever professors with archaeology Ph.D.s did there. Daddy anyway. Mama had just gone along for the ride. They'd be back the day after tomorrow, I realized. And tomorrow could be gone in a heartbeat or two.

"It's not just a sunset," I said, going for poetic. "It's a moonrise, too."

Kieren's nostrils flared at that, which I found exceedingly manly. Besides, I'd always loved this time of day, late evening when the world went smoky and soft. Dusk. Twilight. Such pretty names. We owed something to the night, didn't we?

I tried pressing my newly rounded right boob against his forearm. Even though it was well covered in a sweat-stained T-shirt, even though the temperature had to be over ninety degrees. I had it on good authority that most

INNOCENZA

Lousy idea, us sitting like that on the railroad tracks. If we had had to jump, it would have been a heart-stopping drop to the lake below. But Kieren had said he could hear a train coming from far away, in more than enough time for us to scramble from the middle of the bridge to safety. And I trusted him. Liked him watching out for me, too.

To the west, the fading horizontal clouds had turned a bloody tangerine color, fuzzy and tinged with violet, boys my age were due to go boob crazy at any time. But my hand was all he was interested in.

As the sun melted into the horizon, I stared into the rippling water and decided to take the lead. If Kieren backed off, I'd make like I was joking.

It seemed to take forever, turning my palm until our fingers aligned, rested against one another, ready to intertwine. His face was flushed, moist from the heat, and his expression didn't tell me anything.

Taking a shallow breath, I went for it. There. My fingertips touched the back of his hand. His fingertips touched the back of mine. And he was letting it happen. I was about to say something—I didn't know what—when distant but sure I heard the train.

"Kieren?" I whispered.

I'd distracted him.

A cause for celebration if it hadn't been for the penalty.

His head snapped in the direction of the oncoming threat, the one that would reach me first, and his eyes in the evening light looked flat and yellow. I didn't feel the pain when I first heard the wet crunching, didn't feel it for long even, wicked hot, turning my sweat cold. There was an instant, just one, when I looked down at my hand and felt the blood dripping and realized his nails . . . claws . . . had extended, piercing clear through, five crescent-shaped punctures, catching raw muscle and splintering bone.

"Oh," I said, like that explained everything, and suddenly, the train didn't matter so much anymore. Then the world swirled, faded, took me floating into the darkness.

Fangs Are Us

*Y*ou're nuts!" I exclaimed after swallowing a bite of tender scallops twirled in garlic fettuccine. "My uncle will never sign off on this."

"No, no, not nuts, Quincie," the chef countered in an accented baritone. "Garlic. He said 'Italian.' Change this. Pave that. But still, Italian. So, garlic."

"But Vaggio!"

His triumphant smile let me in on the joke. "Ah, *bambina,* so predictable."

It was nearly 9 P.M., and since sevenish that evening, I'd been playing taste tester for the teasing and tiring chef. Each dish had been sensual, succulent, but none had screamed, "*Presto*: blood lust!" And that's what we were going for.

Sanguini's was to be Austin's first restaurant built around a vampire theme. More class than kitsch, but not without a sense of playfulness. A reboot of Fat Lorenzo's, the family-style Italian restaurant on South Congress that had once belonged to Gramma and Grampa Crimi, who'd left it to Mama. She'd often called the business her "other child" and seemed more at home there than she did in the house.

At least until three winters ago, when she and Daddy died on the icy 183 exit ramp off MoPac Expressway, orphaning me and the restaurant. The will had placed both of us in the care of Daddy's younger brother, Davidson, until I hit twenty-one.

Back then, Uncle D was in his mid-twenties, barely out of Texas State University. I was only fourteen, and the marinara in my veins came from Mama's side of the family, not Daddy's. But Vaggio, the chef who'd known my late grandparents since back in their Chicago days, helped Uncle D get up to speed. And from then on, I spent more time at Fat Lorenzo's than anywhere else, even Kieren's.

All was well until last year when Pasta Perfecto opened a few blocks south. Though our regulars had stayed regular, their parking lot was twice the size of ours. Within six months, Fat Lorenzo's was in the red.

Something had to change, I'd said, or we'd find ourselves out of business. Vaggio had argued that we should stick with Italian, claiming he didn't know how to cook anything else. Uncle Davidson had suggested the vampire concept.

"Can't we just do a ghost?" Vaggio had asked. "It's an old building. We could make up a story, say somebody who worked here died."

"Nah," Uncle Davidson had replied. "Haunted has been done to death."

I didn't know much more about vampires than anyone else. After all, the last reported sighting of one in Texas had been about the time of the Kennedy assassination.

And even though Kieren, my hybrid werewolf best friend, was a self-appointed expert on creatures of the night, he didn't like talking about vampires. He'd once said, though, that it offended him that "the leeches" could turn into something wolflike, too.

"What if some real vampires actually show up?" I'd wanted to know.

"We'll make a fortune" had been my uncle's reply.

In the end, Uncle Davidson's plan had seemed like a bang-up way to keep us all in Chianti. He'd hired a contractor to remodel, expanding into what had once been the vintage threads shop next door. That had doubled the size of the main dining room, offered space for two four-stall *baños*, allowed for a small break room and private dining room, and increased the kitchen square footage by a third.

For most of my fellow Waterloo High School seniors, the future was little more than a misty dream. Mine had a liquor license from the state of Texas and an uncle-manager who'd bailed tonight to go skinny-dipping with his girlfriend, Ruby.

Picking up a menu cover that had been sitting on the stainless steel counter, I studied it once more. White with pinkish blue undertones, made of pressed leather with an impractical gold tassel for trim and hard-to-decipher, gothic-style crimson lettering. The effect—as intended—was a body bled dry and dressed in party clothes.

The interior was empty, though, awaiting Vaggio's frantic efforts to produce one more main course, the appetizers, and desserts. He had five weeks until opening and claimed to work best on deadline.

After a moment, Vaggio plucked the menu from my hands, stepped to a refrigerator, and handed me a small plate of green olives. "Go away. Take this with you to the break room. Your friend—"

"His name is Kieren." I closed my fingers around the cold plate. "Kieren Morales." I wouldn't blush. Girls who wooed werewolves were beyond blushing, and Vaggio had known Kieren forever. He was just telling me without telling me that he had reservations about our relationship.

"Yes, Kieren." Vaggio poured me a glass of water. "Tonight, will you confess your *amore*? To the lucky one you chose as friend?"

Had I been that transparent? Kieren probably knew, but Kieren knew I'd come down with the chicken pox at age four at Disney World and something far more unpleasant at age nine in Ecuador. He knew the first boy I'd kissed was Julio Gutiérrez, in the hall next to the janitor's closet at the eighth grade Spring Fling. He even knew when I started my period, and not just because he could smell it.

"I have plenty of friends."

"Do you?" Vaggio moved to the sink, dropping the Italian accent he'd been practicing for Sanguini's launch party.

"I'm always busy, aren't I?"

"That is true." Vaggio turned back to look at me. He'd given up on suggesting I abandon the restaurant—at least for a few years—in pursuit of my "endangered" youth. But he would urge me, now and then, not to forget I was a teenager. "Fear not, *bambina*. I'll send back Kieren when he arrives."

"*Grazie*," I replied, then paused, uncertain. "Everything's going to work out, isn't it?" I wasn't sure whether I was talking about Sanguini's new menu or what might happen tonight between Kieren and me.

"Are you kidding?" Vaggio extended his arms, king of the kitchen. "This is the life!"

Laughing, I exited the swinging door and crossed the break room to set my snack on the coffee table. The phone beside my glass started ringing. "Hello? Hellllo?" I answered, snagging the receiver. "Howdy?"

With a shrug, I hung up on the dial tone.

Man or Wolf-Man, the Boy Was Mine

I cut the lights and settled on the frayed floral sofa in front of the TV, hitting the remote ON button. The wolf documentary teaser flashed fangs and fur, teeth and tearing, the beastly and the beautiful. It promised mating, after a commercial break.

I sipped my water—the liquid looked black in the near darkness. The only light was from the TV screen. Every window in the historic building had been bricked up during the renovation. I kept the volume low and popped a habanera-stuffed olive into my mouth, pausing to lick my fingers.

Volcanic spice drenched my teeth, tongue, gums.

Zeroing in on the screen, I bit into another olive and shuddered as a wolf snapped her jaws into a rabbit's belly, messing her muzzle and the snow. Then as the British narrator anthropomorphized, I winced at a series of clattering clanks and a half-choked call from the kitchen. "You okay?" I called. "Vaggio?"

No reply.

"Vaggio?"

Still *nada*.

He'd live, I decided, nestling deeper into the sofa. I'd expected Kieren to show by nine at the latest but appreciated the chance to catch part of this documentary. The topic was wolves, the kind who walked on all fours all the time, rather than werewolves (AKA Wolves with the capital *W*), who shape-shifted between that and human form.

I had firsthand knowledge of werewolves. Now, I was looking for hands-on. Call me werecurious, but if my mission was to arouse the boy with the beast within, I'd have to tantalize his monster. And I'd tried. I'd really tried. Over the past couple of months, I'd tried my paper-thin baby-pink tank top, air conditioner cranked, no bra. I'd tried tequila—silver, José Cuervo Clásico, no worm. I'd even tried patience. Considered hypnotherapy. Changed my deodorant. Wondered if something about me was repulsive.

I would've given up ages ago—I had my pride— but Kieren was always touching me. My neck, my shoulders, my hands. I could feel him wanting more.

My lips curled at the TV footage of the female's mate. Grey-black and extra large. I glanced from the clock on the cable box—9:16 P.M.—to the door between me and the kitchen, ate another olive, took another sip. I should've grabbed some bread, I thought, something to absorb the sting.

Onscreen, the wolves were going at it. My water hit a wrong pipe, and I was coughing. It got worse when the scene progressed to wolf pups exploring their new world. But it was funny: the idea of safe sex with a *Canis dirus sapiens*. Wasn't it?

The narrator went on to say wolves had gotten a bum rap from ranchers and tellers of fairie tales. It was the same with shifters, I thought, and those bigots who thought they all should have to be registered and tagged.

As the credits rolled, a wolf's soulful eyes filled the screen. They looked like they knew something I didn't.

"Quince!" It was Kieren from the kitchen. *"Quince!"*

I clicked off the TV and put down my glass and plate. Did I have olive-habanera breath? I wondered. Probably. "Coming!"

"Quince!" Kieren again. *"Quince!* Where are you?"

Alarmed by his tone, I hurried. "On my way!"

When I pushed through the door into the overlit commercial kitchen, Kieren was rushing toward me. "Thank you, Jesus. Thank God."

"What is it? What's wrong?"

Whispering my name, Kieren wrapped me in well-muscled arms, brushed a kiss across my hairline. We fitted well, shoulder-to-shoulder and hip-to-hip. Not a big guy, but a huge Wolf. Or at least he would've been, if he could only fully shape-shift.

"You're all right?" he asked. "You look all right."

Of course I was all right, I thought, blinking at the gleaming stainless steel. The kitchen still smelled like scallops and garlic and marinara but something richer and heavier, too. Something foul.

Over Kieren's shoulder, I saw shards of glass glittering against a red wine spill on the acid-stained concrete floor. A ragged, seeping scrap of meat had been plopped on the wooden butcher's block.

My fingers were red, sticky. It was from touching him. "You're a mess," I said. There was blood on his hands, his Fat Lorenzo's T-shirt, even on his faded jeans and black cowboy boots. "Where's Vaggio?"

Kieren sucked in a breath, moved his hips closer. "We've gotta get out of here."

That's when I saw the disjointed legs lying on the floor, jutting out from behind a prep station. It was partly the dark, irregular pattern on the beige cargo pants and kitchen clogs. It was partly the angle the legs were sprawled at, turned to each other as if for comfort. I smelled blood, urine. "*Vaggio?*"

"We have to *go*. Call somebody."

"But—"

"Don't look, Quince." Kieren held me in place, sweat dotting his forehead, tears in his dark eyes. "I tried to help him. But it was too late."

Twisting out of Kieren's embrace, I crossed the room to see for myself.

Vaggio lay mauled, bleeding, his skin waxy and gaunt. Savaged. Shirt partly torn away. An oozing claw mark raked across his chest. Blood pooling from the carnage where his throat had been.

I'd seen death before, Mama and Daddy in mortician's makeup and their Sunday best. It was different without the staging, different when the person had been ripped apart. What was left wasn't Vaggio anymore. My stomach rolled.

Kieren caught me again as I began to scream. He swept me out of the building to the empty lot next door. Close enough to the street that we were in view of the entertainment district. Far enough away to offer some privacy.

We sank to the warm ground, and he held me, sobbing, folded against his bloodstained T-shirt, his thundering heart. He buried his nose in my hair, rubbing my back, whispering my name.

QUESTIONING

*O*nce I could stand again, Kieren walked me down the street to a nearby motel and used the lobby phone to call 911. I could hear only his end of the conversation.

"Police.

"Kieren Morales.

"K-I-E-R-E-N Morales, with an *s*."

I sank into the lime-upholstered chair next to the window.

"Someone's been killed, the chef at my best friend's family's restaurant.

"Yeah, she's here."

A woman with a spiky blue Mohawk looked from me to Kieren like she was worried he was mistreating me somehow. But then the desk clerk greeted her.

"Upset but okay," Kieren said into the phone.

"We're at the Capitol Motel. We're safe.

"No."

A young guy with a shiny black cowboy shirt and black jeans joined the woman. She whispered something to him, and he glanced our way.

"My friend was in the break room at the restaurant. I walked into the kitchen through the back door and discovered the body.

"Quincie Morris." He spelled "Q-U-I-N-C-I-E."

"Vaggio Bianchi." He spelled both names. So calm. Like when my folks died. Like when his mama went into labor with Meghan. Almost inhuman.

I closed my eyes against the memory of claw marks.

"Yes," Kieren said, "the chef."

He went on to describe the kitchen and say that an ambulance wouldn't help.

Within five minutes they'd sent an ambulance anyway along with two police cars. I didn't get a chance to talk to EMS, but back in Sanguini's parking lot,

Officer Walker and Officer Rodriguez of the Austin Police Department introduced themselves.

Officer Walker ushered us to a squad car, away from curious passersby. We huddled in the back seat, and the cop took a moment to study us before shutting the door. Kieren had already explained he was bloody from trying to help, that I was bloody from touching him. He put his arm around my shoulders, and I cradled his free hand with both of mine, studying the dark stains against his skin.

"I was just in the next room," I whispered.

"I know."

I tightened my grip. "Do you think the killer is still in there?"

"I don't know."

The front passenger door opened, and I saw yellow police tape unfurling.

Officer Walker joined us in the car, asked some basic questions.

"I'd like to take her home," Kieren said after a lull. "Is that all?"

"No, we'll need you both downtown."

Outside, APD cameras flashed.

I didn't know what time it was when we got to the station, but when I called, Uncle D still wasn't home.

Officer Walker used the moment to separate me from Kieren. Then he introduced Detective Bartok and said she had more questions.

"Where's Kieren?" I asked, taking a seat in a private room.

"He's fine," Detective Bartok replied, pressing a button on a tape recorder. "You're good friends?"

Jesus. "Yeah."

"How good?"

I stared at her, blank.

"We'll come back to that. How 'bout you tell me what happened tonight?"

It was her job to help catch the killer, I reminded myself. "I'd been helping out Vag, *Vaggio* tonight in the kitchen. He's, he was trying to put together a new menu for the restaurant. It's reopening soon, and . . . Anyway, Kieren was supposed to meet me there, and I went into the break room to watch TV and wait for him while Vaggio finished up. I never would've left him if . . . It doesn't matter. While I was watching television—"

"What were you watching?"

The wolf documentary. I blinked back the memory, what had looked like an animal attack. What was Kieren being asked? "I, um, I don't remember."

"Take a moment. Think about it."

I did. "I was channel surfing, I guess."

"And?"

"I heard a couple of noises, like pans being banged around, and I yelled to ask Vaggio if he was okay." Had the murderer heard me? He must've. "I didn't think . . . I *never* imagined that anything like that could happen. Then Kieren got there and he was calling my name and I went into the kitchen and then I saw. . . . That was it. Kieren led me out, and we went to call—"

"What is your relationship to Mr. Morales?"

I'd wondered myself. "We're friends."

"Do your parents know you're out this late?"

"They're dead," I said, wiping away a tear.

"I'm sorry." She looked at her notepad. "Oh, yes. Your uncle, Davidson Morris, is your legal guardian. Does he know where you are?"

"I wasn't able to get ahold of him."

"That's no problem. You're seventeen. We consider that an adult."

It dawned on me that I might be a suspect, not just a witness. "I loved Vaggio," I said, glancing at the red light on the recorder. "He was like family."

Detective Bartok offered a brief, respectful silence. Then she said, "Speaking of family, I'm curious about your genetic history. What hospital were you born in?"

Cursing myself for having been caught off guard, I almost asked if I should be calling a lawyer. Or if Kieren should be.

It was common knowledge that werepeople—be they Wolves, Deer, Buffalo, Raccoons, whatever—were never treated in hospitals. Wolf packs had their own doctors, probably even their own clinics. Lone Wolves, like Kieren's mama, used midwives or volunteer home-visit docs, all of them shifters, too. She herself had apprenticed as a healer before leaving her pack, which was why I still had use of my scarred hand.

I clenched it, telling myself that whoever the murderer had been, it wasn't Kieren. I knew him. I'd known him all my life. "Seton Medical Center," I said. "On Thirty-eighth Street."

The detective made a note.

RESTAURANTS

Sanguini's: A Very Rare Restaurant
is hiring a *chef de cuisine*. Dinners
only. Apply in person between 2
and 4 P.M. M–F. Ask for Davidson
Morris, head manager.

Every Dog Has His Day

I didn't know Vaggio had had five ongoing love affairs until all the women showed up for his memorial service.

Uncle Davidson had kept it simple, spiritual, and settled for an outdoor thing at the top of Mount Bonnell because the real funeral would be up north anyway. Vaggio's family had flown down Nancy, a first cousin, to sort through his belongings and drive the Lincoln back to Chicago. She was the one accepting sympathies.

My uncle and his girlfriend, Ruby, were off to the side making inappropriate lusty goo-goo eyes at each other. Kieren was patting the hand of a sweet, sixtysomething lady named Daniela who'd exploded into tears. Kieren's parents would've come, but Roberto was keynoting at some engineering faculty conference in Ann Arbor and Meara couldn't find a sitter for Meghan. It was still a good turnout though. Vaggio's neighbors, his poker buddies, several former Fat Lorenzo's employees, and Detective Bartok with another cop whose name I'd already spaced off.

I soaked in the sun, shuffling my feet on the limestone, trying to appreciate the sweeping views of downtown and the lake. The cacti, the sage.

Vaggio had brought me here once, three years ago, the day he'd said that my uncle might be the one with legal custody, but he too would always be there for me. We'd hiked up the uneven stairs to the top of the park, where stone had been crafted to look like the ruins of an ancient temple. He'd led me to this bench and said, "Close your eyes, and feel that God is with us." I had felt God then, so I closed my eyes and tried again.

Where was God today?

At the sound of laughter, I glared at my uncle in one of his typical Hawaiian shirts and his girlfriend in a plunging black dress. Then Ruby laughed again, louder, and everybody looked her way.

She hadn't known Vaggio well, and she was a disturbing personality.

Ruby (not her real name, I suspected) Kitahara was a living vampire. Not someone infected with vampirism but a human, a wannabe who'd taken tartare too far. Uncle D loved her. Or at least she was the first woman he'd slept with for more than two consecutive weeks. "Woman" being a stretch. I was seventeen, and she was three, four years older than me. As for my baby-faced uncle, lately he might've been far from Mr. Maturity, but he was still pushing thirty.

Uncle D adjusted his shades and strolled over. "You ready to go?"

I shook my head. "I can catch a ride."

"With Kieren?" He'd started treating Kieren like a potential niece defiler about the time we hit adolescence.

"Yeah."

Uncle D gave me a hug and told me he loved me for the tenth time that day.

Once he and Ruby had left, Kieren joined me on the bench and introduced Daniela and Vaggio's other lady friends, Celeste, Emilia, Gladys, and LaShauna.

After the initial shock, they'd taken the news of each

others' existence better than most women would, had decided to go out together for margaritas that evening. They all had something to say to me, too. "He loved you." "Talked about you all the time." "Light of his life." "Pride and joy." "Granddaughter he never had."

I mustered up a smile as they joined arms to belt out "Strangers in the Night," Vaggio's signature song. His last gift to me, those women, and just when I needed them. It was funny, though, the things you didn't learn about people until after they died.

Kieren and I stayed after Vaggio's cousin Nancy had gone, kissing each of us on the cheek and promising that Vaggio's sausage lasagna would be served after his formal funeral. We camped out on the bench I'd chosen earlier, watching the sun glint against the lake.

I felt guilty about the flashes of suspicion I'd had the night Vaggio died. After all, Kieren was half human, too, and I probably wouldn't have suspected him at all if it had looked from the crime scene like the murderer was *Homo sapiens.*

"Is it any less bad?" Kieren asked.

The grief, he meant. It was. Not better. But less bad.

"Quince, I hate to bring this up now, but there's a chance the murderer might—"

"Don't talk about that. Not here."

"Where then?"

"It's . . . I get that the police can only do so much." I straightened. "When I go back to the restaurant, I'm taking Grampa Crimi's .45 with me."

I didn't know how to hold a gun, let alone aim and shoot. But maybe I could use it to scare someone.

"No way in hell," Kieren said, and that caught my attention. He wasn't the one of us inclined to cuss. "Somebody could use it against you. And even if you were a trained sharpshooter, I don't think a gun would help."

God. "Could we talk about this later?"

"Quince, you're just—"

"I'm scared, okay?" I broke his gaze. *"Okay?"*

"Okay."

Okay. "I love you, you know," I said, by way of apology. A day like this, I could tell him, and it was less risky. More about us as friends.

His answer was to wrap his arms around me, bring my head to his shoulder, my side to his chest. Touching. He was touching me again. I could feel his breath, hear in it something that might've been a whisper, a "Yes."

BLOOD RELATIONS

I set the hammer beside my planner book on the hostess stand and hung Vaggio's framed photo next to those of my parents and grandparents and the first dollar ever earned at Fat Lorenzo's. There, I thought. The pictures didn't fit the décor, but so what. No matter what we called the place or how we changed the interior design, this was still a family establishment. My family's establishment.

Besides, it was a great shot. Vaggio grinning like a fool on his sixty-fifth birthday. It had been last fall, the week before Thanksgiving. I could remember him say-ing retirement was for wimps. I straightened the frame.

Sinatra himself had never looked better.

Vaggio's murder had been almost a week earlier, his memorial service two days ago, and I could barely remember what life had been like before. It reminded me of losing Mama and Daddy. Everything's good, or at least normal, and then, in an instant, nothing would ever be the same.

"Honey, don't take this wrong," Uncle D said, joining me in the foyer to study my handiwork, "but Vaggio—and you know how much I'll miss him—wasn't family. Not really. This is a nice gesture, but—"

"He was family to Mama and me," I said. "And Daddy adored him."

It was my big gun, invoking Daddy. I didn't do it often.

"But Vaggio wasn't blood," Uncle D surprised me by insisting. "Not that it may matter anyway. After all that's happened, we may be better off renting out the building to some other restaurant."

"You can't be serious!" I exclaimed, packing up the hammer and the rest of the nails in the toolbox. Granted, Uncle D had been under a lot of pressure before Vaggio's death. It made sense that he felt overwhelmed now. But we'd already lost so much. No way would I give up the restaurant, too.

"Commercial real estate has soared on South Congress," he argued. "Given the breakeven or worse prospects on Sanguini's, it might be more profitable to collect the rent." He moved toward the photo of my parents, touched the glass over Daddy's face. "Besides, there's so much to be done between now and the opening. Without Vaggio, I don't know how I'll be able to pull it all off."

"I can help," I told him. I'd always helped. Answered phones, took reservations, seated guests, bused tables, restocked, mopped, dumped trash, whatever. "*Really* help," I clarified. "Like with management stuff. What do you need me to do most?"

I already had Frank, my day planner, open and ready to record to-dos.

Uncle D turned from my parents' photo to study me for a long moment. "You're sure this is what you want, to be entombed in this old place?"

"It's home," I said.

"Home," Uncle D repeated. He thought for a moment and then snapped his fingers. "Well, for starters, I'm putting you in charge of the new chef."

That was weird, I thought, especially since we didn't even have a new chef yet. The whole idea sounded suspiciously like busywork, something to keep me out of the way. "Wouldn't a chef already know what to do?"

"Hopefully," Uncle D agreed. "But you'll help him out, keep me posted on any problems. The chef is key to the whole operation. In the end, our future rests in his hands."

Fine. I'd hover on Uncle D's behalf, if only so he could concentrate on everything else. "But what about the relaunch, the whole Sanguini's experience? I want something about the place to have my personal touch."

Something to make Mama proud, I thought. She'd been a perfectionist, critical sometimes, but that was because she cared so much. She understood how her parents had sacrificed, coming from Italy, building their business from smarts and sweat. That's why she spent so much time at Fat Lorenzo's instead of at the house. She wanted to leave something for me.

"We'll see what develops," Uncle D said. "In the meantime, you'll have to really buckle down. Stop running off with your friends so much."

Kieren, he meant.

BLOOD PRESSURE

"Sanguini's: A Very Rare Restaurant," I mumbled into the phone, annoyed that another call had slipped through before I could figure out how to reprogram the automatic answering message. "Hello?" I glanced at the digital clock radio on top of the office desk. It was already a quarter till 7 P.M. "Hell—"

"Good evening," greeted an affected voice that sounded more like Count Chocula than Count Dracula. "I just flew in from Transylvania—"

"And your wings are so tired."

Hanging up, I relaxed into the chair across from my uncle's desk. The restaurant would debut at sundown Friday, September 13. That in mind, I winced first at the calendar—Thursday, August 15—and then at the résumés spitting out of the fax machine.

"Anything promising?" I asked.

Uncle Davidson's smile was a weary one. While I'd been fielding media, crank, and reservations calls, he'd been sorting the chef applications into piles: die-hard goths, fast-food rejects, one-year-plus unemployed, and some woman who claimed Vaggio's ghost had appeared to her in a dream. Since we'd had no promising local applicants, Uncle D had posted the chef-wanted ad on a few free job-seeker websites, but he'd provided the restaurant fax number instead of requesting e-submissions. *Big* mistake.

"This one doesn't look bad," he said, holding up a piece of paper. "I'll call his references and set up an interview."

Ruby sauntered into the office, sporting, per usual, a sheer, long-sleeve black dress—feather neck and feather-trimmed sleeve cuffs—over a low-cut, laced leather bustier, black leather pants, and clunky, knee-high boots, each fastened with five oversize silver buckles. Her Morticia-streaked shiny black hair swung low to a microscopic waistline, and she'd gone heavy on the eyeliner. A deep violet, it clashed with her dilated green eyes.

The first twenty-four hours after Vaggio's death, Uncle Davidson had put *her* in front of the TV cameras. Ruby had managed to pull off confident, in command, sensitive, and low-key creepy in a heartbeat. Hers had been the face on page one of the *Statesman,* the *Chronicle,* the *Cap City News, USA Today,* the recurring clip on CNN. When coiffed heads from Concerned Mothers for America's Children victim-blamed us for Vaggio's murder on round-the-clock cable news, Ruby was their prime example of "the demented freaks swarming our cities."

A lone murder in a southwestern college town wouldn't normally have merited national coverage. But toss in the restaurant's theme and the fact that this was the state capital. . . . They were calling it "The Texas Vampire Murder."

I'd been doing all I could to tune out the coverage since the first time I'd heard the words "medical-legal autopsy."

"Guess what," Ruby said with childlike delight.

"What?" Uncle D indulged.

"Some guys have set up a table out front. They're asking people to sign a petition giving amnesty to killer vampires."

"They're what?" I asked.

When the *Chronicle* first reported Sanguini's would have a vampire theme, we'd gotten a couple of concerned calls from BADL (the Bat Anti-Defamation League). Austin was home to the world's largest urban bat colony, and BADL had been worried about possible PR fallout. Like we'd ever besmirch the city's most treasured eco-mascots. The point being, political activism was huge here, but this was ridiculous.

"They're outside our front door?" Uncle D wanted to know.

She nodded like it was the niftiest thing ever.

Sprinting from the back office, down the hall, I followed my uncle past the restroom doors and kitchen door, through the crimson velvet curtains, across the dining room, and through another matching set of curtains to the foyer to pull back a final set of curtains that hung in front of the painted black door. Overkill, designed to tap into the popular idea that sunlight destroyed vampires. No more than a myth, Kieren had told me once. False comfort. In any case, a small, beveled, oval-shaped window had been cut into the door. Uncle D and I took turns peering through it.

Six, no seven, young melanin-challenged guys dressed in black long sleeves, long pants, and shades were perched on the sidewalk in foldout lawn chairs beneath black umbrellas, drinking what I hoped was cherry Kool-Aid out of clear plastic cups. A card table had been set up in front of them. It was so stupid. So incredibly disrespectful.

It would serve them all right if they had heat stroke.

"If this keeps up," Uncle D said, "the other merchants will start bitching. They're already nervous."

The neighborhood association had asked for more of a police presence, and in the past few days, I'd spotted more bicycle officers and squad cars than usual.

"I don't blame them," I replied.

Letting the curtains fall into place, Uncle D used the hostess station phone to call APD. I excused myself to take refuge at Kieren's.

THE FACTS OF LIFE

*F*our years ago, the Moraleses leveled their 1920s three-bedroom bungalow to build a white stone and stucco two-story with a soaring foyer and a finished bonus room that Kieren's parents shared as a home office. The place was roomy, took up most of the lot, your basic McMansion. The neighbors had hissy fits.

The front yard was rocked except for a wild rose garden that always seemed to be in bloom, and Meghan's tire swing hung from the winding branch of a live oak.

When the door opened, giant paws landed on my shoulders, knocking me back a step. I shut my eyes against the enthusiastic tongue. Brazos was Kieren's dog, a shepherd, silver and white with smoky brown eyes. Sporting his royal blue bandanna.

"Hey, boy! Down, down." And when he went back to all fours, I crouched beside him, wrapping my arms around his neck, pressing my face into the warm fur, inhaling his dog smell. Everybody had seemed different since Vaggio died, but not Brazos.

I smiled up at Kieren's mama. "Howdy."

"Come on in. Kieren's upstairs, studying. Can I get you some water?" She led me in, and Brazos trailed after us, tail wagging. "We also have Diet Coke, orange juice, Dr Pepper, lemonade, iced tea—"

"Dr Pepper, please." I made my way through the foyer, past the stairs, to the great room.

It was sterile. White walls and moldings and doors and Berber carpeting. Framed bluebonnet and Indian paintbrush photos. Furniture via Pottery Barn and Everything Leather. University of Texas Longhorns pillows on the sofa. Oaxacan wood carvings on the mantle of a never-used fireplace.

Like most werepeople, Mama Wolf and her cubs were firmly in the closet—or, well, den—and the house was part of the illusion. So much depended on it—

their safety, Meghan's playdates, Kieren's presumed innocence, Dr. Morales's job at the U., Miz Morales's Junior League bridal clientele.

She excused herself to fetch my drink and feed the dog.

Perching on the cushy white leather couch, I turned my attention to the coffee table. It was littered with powder blue and navy earrings assembled from ribbons, mesh, and satin rosebuds. I picked one up. "Yowza."

"Hideous, aren't they?" Miz Morales asked, returning with my drink—pink glass tumbler, heart-shaped ice, and moss-colored cotton napkin. "The bride is the daughter of oil-money Houstonians, the groom the son of dot-com investors who got out in time."

She loved to dish, and it was fun listening, though little of her Irish accent remained. I wasn't sure why her family had relocated—or had been relocated here during her childhood—but Kieren had told me once that they were descended from Wolves who'd known St. Patrick himself.

I'd teased him that it was the ultimate in blarney, but the story reminded me of Daddy, how he always used to talk about my being named for some great, great (I didn't know how many greats) uncle. A Texas war hero.

I played with my straw. "You'll make it work," I told Miz Morales. "Somehow."

She had the magic touch. Nobody could do a better job of talking a nice girl and her mama out of a regrettable ice sculpture.

"Quincie," Miz Morales said, taking a step back. "It's been hard for you, at your age, without Gate and Sophie."

Just like that. *Bam*. No segue. They'd all been friends, though, my parents and Kieren's, back in their college days. Stood up in each others' weddings.

"I know your uncle tries. Still, Roberto and I should've done more. Now that you're a young woman, I realize . . . Well, I hope you'll accept my apologies."

I sipped my Dr Pepper, confused.

"It's time a woman explained to you the facts of life."

Oh, God. "Miz Morales, with all respect, I don't think—"

"Has Kieren talked to you yet about what it means, what will happen . . . ?"

Ah, got it. "Big Bad Wolf to-do," I replied, even more tense at the subject clarification. "Sooner or later, he'll be in or out of the pack of his choice."

I was hazy on the details, but supposedly, there were two ways into a Wolf pack: brains or brawn. Kieren was very strong—stronger and faster than any

100 percent human but not as strong or fast as a 100 percent Wolf—so he'd be applying, or whatever prospective members did, on the first count—hence his extensive werestudies.

I had a nagging feeling he'd be better off with more tooth and claw to back up that noggin power, and what's more, I wasn't sold on the idea that a Wolf pack would embrace a hybrid. But Kieren never seemed concerned, and he'd told me more than once to stop worrying about it.

"At eighteen," Miz Morales said, circling the couch, "as a human, he'd have to register for the draft. As a Wolf, it's not much different."

"Are you sure that's a good idea if he can't . . . ?"

Full-blooded werepeople could shift at will, but it became harder to keep from going full puppy when the moon went fat. Miz Morales never took a wedding booked on such dates nor met then with her clients. But Kieren had never fully transformed, and the one time he'd gone halfway had been a disaster for us both.

It wasn't something his parents had known to expect. Full werepeople never shifted at all before adolescence, and hybrids were virtually unheard of.

Or at least not talked about.

So it wasn't clear whether Kieren would *ever* be able to transform completely.

"I left my pack, Quincie." She sank to sit on her heels in front of me. "Left it because I was young and idealistic and I believed love was all that mattered. As much as I treasure Roberto and the kids, living free of the hierarchy, we're making do with a loose network of other runaways, outcasts, antisocials. It's like a Band-Aid when only full body armor will do. Kieren needs a pack. Most lone Wolves don't survive long."

"Kieren may be half Wolf . . ." I set the ice-cold tumbler on the sofa table. "But he's also half *Homo sapiens.*" Besides, he wasn't alone. He had his family. He had me.

Miz Morales stood, reaching to scratch behind her ear. "Please understand. I'd hoped this could wait until graduation, at least Christmas break. But the way things are going . . ." She stilled. "'Sooner or later' could mean any time. And it's not like he'd be able to come back and visit. You, me, Roberto, Meghan—we can't be selfish. We have to let him go."

Forever? I'd never realized that Kieren's joining a pack would mean he'd be gone for good. I'd just thought it was . . . I don't know . . . like the Army

Reserve or something. In peacetime. Kieren had never hinted that his being half Wolf could lead to this.

I opened my mouth to protest as Miz Morales glanced at her watch.

"Oh, no!" she exclaimed.

"What?" I asked, fretting what else might be wrong.

"I'm supposed to be meeting with the Jung-Holland bride at the Driskill Hotel." She smoothed her tailored skirt. "Ms. Jung wanted to release doves until I explained how last time I did that four out of the twelve flew into a passing semi, so now we're leaning toward butterflies." Miz Morales moved closer again, brushed my hair from my eyes. "So much of Sophie in you," she said. "I'm sorry, but I've got to run. Roberto's at a faculty dinner at U.T., so you kids are on your own tonight."

I found my voice. "Miz Morales," I began, "Kieren can't leave. He belongs—"

"Be strong, Quincie," she said, "for Kieren's sake."

Twice Shy

Upstairs, Kieren was setting *Where the Wild Things Are* on his nightstand. Meghan lay cradled, sleeping in his arms. "Let me tuck her in," he whispered, rising to carry his sister off to bed.

If you turned Kieren into a four-year-old girl, he'd look like Meghan. Hair so brown it was almost black, so thick and curly it could make a shampoo model weep with envy. Brows barely parted, the shadow of a mustache. She was barefoot, her feet curled, softly snoring, wearing footie PJs. Sweet. A scar ran down her dimpled face, though, forehead to chin, splitting her generous right eyebrow, cutting into the lid and a downy cheek. A souvenir from a break-in when Meghan was a babe.

Burglar, Kieren had said. His mama had handled it.

Left alone, I made an effort to calm myself and searched for a place to sit. Kieren's room was a Wolf studies hot zone. On the top of his water bed, a number of yellowed maps and dusty texts had been spread. Various pages marked with color-coded Post-its. Sometimes I thought he was even more of a workaholic than I was.

Turning, I noticed the plate of desiccated baby-back ribs on the desk.

Kieren's computer monitor displayed an online shopping cart, and I wandered over to peruse the selections: mustard seed, buckthorn, candles, carrot seeds, crosses, crucifixes, Stars of David, Prayer Wheels, Prayer Flags, bells, gongs, dried red peppers, holy water and wafers, dehumidifiers . . . A gold card in the name of Roberto Morales lay on the desk beside an Austin Ice Bats coffee mug, filled with mechanical pencils, highlighters, and pens.

Two empty beer cans had been tossed into the trash. Coors, the Silver Bullet. Kieren's brew of choice and his warped idea of a joke. The brand reminded me of another time, not long before Meghan was born, when we'd been left home alone.

"This way," Kieren had said that day, gesturing for me to follow.

His folks would be back any moment from running errands, and whatever it was, Kieren had wanted to show it to me before they returned.

He'd opened a door in the bungalow ceiling, pulled down a ladder to the attic.

And I'd followed him up, perplexed by the boring landscape of boxes, an artificial Christmas tree, an antique trunk, and a shelf filled with paperback romances. "So?"

"So, *this*." Kieren reached above a support beam stretched across the low, pitched ceiling to grab a key and used it to open a desk drawer.

My eyes widened, sure he wasn't allowed to do that.

Kieren grinned as if he were about to reveal a pirate's treasure, reached into the drawer, and retrieved a folder labeled "silver merchandising."

My first thought had been that Miz Morales had gone into the jewelry business to supplement her bridal planning, but then Kieren handed me a piece of paper.

"You know how we thought silver bullets might be

the only kind that could kill me?" he'd asked. "Look! We were wrong. Any bullet can. Wolves have just been telling people since forever that only silver works to figure out who's after one of us."

According to the document, werewolves sold silver bullets, silver knives, silver spearheads and arrowheads and tracked whoever bought them. The theory was to cut off the enemy at the weapons-supply point. The downside? To maintain the scam, they couldn't nab the villain on premises. Instead, an undercover Wolf followed the trail and dealt with the buyer off-site.

I was impressed by the Wolves' self-defense, but upset that it was necessary to protect people like Kieren and his family. I didn't have a chance to say anything, though. The Moraleses had just arrived downstairs, and Kieren's mama called to us.

He grabbed the document from my hands, slipped it back in the folder, the folder into the drawer, locking and then hurrying to return the key.

When we'd climbed downstairs, Miz Morales had been waiting. Eight months pregnant in a Texas July. Cranky. "I told you to stay out of there."

That night the attic had been locked with a key Kieren never found. The following month, Meghan was born, and then Kieren and I had our accident on the railroad bridge.

Kieren had a sort of split personality, he'd explained. Man and Wolf. Except his Wolf couldn't fully come forth, which frustrated and angered it. Like an abused animal, made it nearly impossible to rein in. Where his mama could shift back and forth whenever, Kieren had barely regained control in time to save me from bleeding to death.

Afterward, his Wolf heritage wasn't our adventure anymore. It was his burden.

Meanwhile, the Morales house was leveled, and, during a year of construction, their newly expanded family made do with a crowded rental and a downtown storage locker. Kieren seemed increasingly too absorbed in his studies to make time for me.

That spring, I kissed someone else, and it tasted like nothing.

For a time, I thought I'd lost Kieren, but the following winter my parents died and he was right by my side. He'd more or less stayed there ever since.

"You hungry?" Kieren asked, drawing my attention back to the present as he rejoined me in his room.

He was always hungry. I lifted *Malleus Maleficarum* from the water bed, trying to sound normal. "I thought you said this was God-awful sexist."

"Sexist, anyway," he acknowledged.

Then . . . it was weird. Kieren gestured as if to

offer me his desk chair but then dropped his hands like he'd changed his mind. I took a couple of steps closer, pausing, unsure whether he would welcome a hug.

We didn't have time to figure it out. I reached for him, and he froze for a moment. But then he relaxed, his gaze softened. My hand hovered in midair. I let it fall. We swayed, nose-to-nose on the white Berber. He wanted to kiss me, didn't he? God only knew I wanted to kiss him.

"My mother—"

"Went to have a little talk about the birds and the butterflies."

"Meghan—"

"Sleeping."

"Papa—"

"At U.T."

"Brazos—"

"I don't think Brazos would mind." I could hear the dog in the backyard, barking like crazy. Miz Morales must've let him out before she left.

I leaned in, but Kieren did this back-step dodge, a sort of nonavoidance avoidance maneuver. Stung, I began, "Unless, you . . ."

His foot nudged a book on the carpet. Damn sheepish for a Wolf.

I retreated, tripping over a yellow highlighter, landing in a sprawl on the sloshing water bed, knocking off three or four priceless ancient texts. I felt myself flush, humiliated. "I, I wasn't trying to—"

"Quince." He took my hand, pulling me up to sit, wavering a bit, on the denim comforter. "It's not you. You're . . . I just . . . I don't want to hurt you."

A werewolf bite could kill. Big jaws, big teeth, big claws like with Grandma and Little Red. But it couldn't make me into a wereperson. Wolves were born, not made. Natural. Not spooky, not demonic, no matter what The Right Wing might say. I tried teasing him, ran my thumb across the back of his hand. "I might enjoy being bitten."

Kieren didn't reply. He let go of me and crossed to his window to check on Brazos, who was still making a lot of racket. Stayed quiet too long. Changed the subject with a whisper. "I think vampires killed Vaggio," he said.

WATCH DOG

"Um, Kieren," I began, choking up. "I was in the kitchen. It looked like—"

"A werewolf kill." He ran a hand through his thick hair. "Yeah, I know. I was there, too. But that's just it. In a Wolf attack, we go for the nose, the buttocks . . . the throat *only* in the case of smaller prey. And, this may not sound pretty, but we don't leave much of anything behind. What happened to Vaggio, it was staged to fit a human misconception, a Hollywood misconception about Wolf behavior. Besides, humans aren't prey. They're our natural enemies. They're to be avoided."

Said the half Wolf to his human best friend.

I crossed my arms, exasperated. "What about vampires?"

"They're dead people too selfish to lie down. There's nothing natural about them."

I felt adrift on the water bed. "So, you're saying a vampire shifted —"

"Changed. *We* shift. *They* change."

Whatever. "*Changed* into a wolf, mauled Vaggio, and then . . . shrank . . . dissolved into mist . . . just before you arrived?"

"Exactly. Quince, the restaurant, the new theme is dangerous."

I stiffened as I realized what he was getting at. "You're saying Sanguini's is attracting real, homicidal vampires? That it's Sanguini's fault, my family restaurant's fault that Vaggio was murdered? That now Vaggio is going to turn into a vampire or something?"

"No, Vaggio's . . . he's dead, not undead." Kieren went into lecture mode. "It takes about a month after first exposure — by ingestion or transfusion of vampire blood — for a human being to become one. Werepeople can't be turned, though, so —"

"You know," I said, rising from the denim comforter, "I road-tripped to the outlet mall in San Marcos last week with Uncle D, and there was this interview on the radio about vampires. I didn't want to listen to it, but he did and, anyway, it was about how they're so low-profile in modern times because they don't have to hunt anymore. They can buy blood or pilfer it. And it's not like they're—"

"Animals?" he asked.

"I was going to say 'eager for attention,'" I replied.

"Look, they've managed to manipulate humans for centuries."

"Will you *shut up* about the goddamned vampires?"

"They are," Kieren said, "damned." He pinched the bridge of his nose, calming himself. "I'm sorry. Of course you're upset—"

"I'm upset because your mama just told me that you'll be leaving soon to join a Wolf pack. Leaving your family. Leaving me. Leaving forever." There, I said it.

Kieren didn't meet my eyes. "A pack is not a prison."

Funny, that's not what it had sounded like downstairs.

He had a map of the Western Hemisphere mounted on his wall, various cities marked by color-coded pins.

Was that where he was going? I wondered. Someplace marked with a pin?

"You've been holding back on us," I said, "because you're leaving. You've known all along, haven't you?"

The five feet from me to him, littered with Wolf lore, seemed like a gulf.

"I belong with a pack, Quince."

"You belong with—"

"I could *kill* you! Don't you get that? I almost did kill you once."

"You wouldn't!" My voice softened. "You won't. I, I trust you."

"I want you to be safe," Kieren countered. "Safe from me, safe from everything bad in the world. Why can't you understand that? Yes, I'm leaving. That's about me, not you. I guess . . . I don't trust myself. If I shift and lose control, a Wolf pack can handle that. You can't. I was going to tell you—"

"When?"

He raised a finger, turned his head. "I hear some-one outside."

How could he hear anything over Brazos? The dog was going ballistic.

Kieren brushed past me. "Stay with Meghan."

"Wait!" I called.

But he was gone. It was amazing how fast he could move.

I jogged down the hall to check on the cub.

Meghan was curled up in her wicker bedroom, her white sheets and waffle-weave blanket kicked off. I pulled one sheet over her, swept curly bangs from her warm forehead, turned on her ceiling fan. It wasn't a fever. Werepeople had a higher body temperature than humans, most of the mammals anyway.

Meghan twisted, nostrils flaring, settling deeper into sleep. My familiar scent had reassured her. She pulled Otto, her toy white rabbit, closer to her chest. For just a moment, it reminded me of the wolf documentary I'd seen the night of Vaggio's murder. The blood-covered muzzle, raw chunks of prey. Then I noticed Meghan's collection of Barbie dolls, lined up on a shelf. Not one in need of electrolysis.

After five minutes or so, Brazos quieted, and I decided it couldn't hurt to peek outside. I couldn't see anything from the upstairs windows, though, so I crept downstairs and opened the front door.

Kieren and Brazos looked alike in posture, poised on the front step, their noses to the wind. "Male," Kieren said. "Smelled like some kind of spice. Gone now, I think."

On more than one occasion, Kieren had confided to me that being half human meant that his senses weren't quite Wolf-sharp, or at least not as sharp as his mama's. I looked around, trying to see, smell for myself. Heat, humidity, somebody barbecuing. Meghan's tire swing flew in the wind.

"Or maybe it was a she . . . ?" Kieren trailed off. "Or a Cat?"

"A cat?" I asked.

"Dogs and Cats don't get along."

THE SCENE OF THE CRIME

*H*iring staff had been a no-brainer, already handled for the most part before Vaggio's death. The vast majority—the pastry team, prep and line cooks, bartenders, servers, and busers—had worked here when it was generic Italian and fang-free.

In strategic makeup and the retro Euro duds Uncle Davidson had bought at All the World's a Stage, every last one could entice the soul from B. B. King or lure Elvis back into the building.

All Uncle D needed them to do was hock food and liquor. Trouble was, with no chef, neither food nor liquor had been lined up for the hocking.

Uncle Davidson's monitoring of incoming applications had revealed that hardly anyone viable wanted to replace Vaggio while his killer was still at large.

I took a breath and held it until I felt the burn. At the moment, Kieren and the headlines kept talking about vampires. From the questions Detective Bartok had asked me, it seemed like the cops suspected a shifter, which didn't necessarily mean they were ruling anyone or anything out. It could've been a human, playing on prejudice against werepeople. It could've been anybody. Nobody knew yet what had happened.

At the back door to the restaurant, the same one the murderer likely used, that thought prompted me to glance over each shoulder, keys clenched tight in my fist, their jagged and pointy metal bodies sticking out like claws from between my curled fingers.

That Friday night, the parking lot was full of pickups, sports cars, two rather cute side-by-side purple PT Cruisers, and a red VW bug painted with black polka dots whose owners had all ignored the Sanguini's PARKING ONLY sign.

At the tiny turquoise-and-pink cottage on the nearest cross street, two men — longtime neighborhood hippies—sat in rocking chairs, smoking weed on their front porch, jamming to classic Willie Nelson and the tinkle of wind chimes. I could hear their voices, but not what they were saying. Could they be inhuman? Could they be talking about me?

A German shepherd—bigger than Brazos—lay curled on the walk leading to their entry stairs, his jaws open and panting. Was he really a dog? I wondered. Was that what Kieren would look like if he could fully shift?

Half past 8 P.M. seemed safe in theory, but . . .

No matter. I'd volunteered to get into the office to register at every single help-wanted website on the Internet. The pay kind that supposedly would get results Uncle Davidson's freebies hadn't. I couldn't do it at home. I'd left both my day planner and my laptop in the office. That's where I normally did my homework and my *work* work.

I had considered waiting until the next day. But it was already Friday, August 16, counting down fast to Friday, September 13's debut party, and if that wasn't bad enough, this Monday would be the first day of school. Best to get in the queue ASAP.

I jammed the oversize key into the lock, and the force pushed the door open a crack. Unlocked, I realized. Light on. A radio piped out Eartha Kitt at top volume.

Still standing on the outside step, I swallowed hard, thought fast. Uncle Davidson had the one other key, and he'd left home over three hours ago to take Ruby to a Death Jam concert in San Antonio.

Still, someone was in the kitchen.

I inched the door closed, maneuvering the knob to mute the latch as it slid back into place. Then, barrier restored, I exhaled, and that's when the huge, filthy hand landed on my shoulder and squeezed.

With a yelp, I jumped aside, revealing a sixty plus man, tanned skin, gaunt and scabby, tobacco seeding his left jawline, peering at me with blue eyes that twinkled like Santa's. He was carrying a hand-lettered, dirty cardboard sign. It read:

GAY REPUBLICAN
WICCAN VETERAN
NEEDS LUV & $

"Mitch!" I whispered, checking the door. "God, don't sneak up on people!"

"Quincie, Quincie, I, I, sweetie pie, I was just seeing if you needed a hand."

Mitch and I looked after each other. Had for years.

"S'okay," I said, filling him in on what I'd discovered as we both sneaked next door. "Did you see anybody?"

"No, nope, didn't see. Been down at the hike-and-bike trail, watching the ducks swim, swimming ducks, on the lake. Swans, too! It sparkled, sparkled so nice today, that lake did. Came on back up the hill. Sor, Sorry."

"Don't worry about it. I'm calling the cops."

"Then I gotta go, if you'll be, if you're gonna be—"

"I'll be fine." Truth was, I wished he'd stick around until the police got there, but it seemed selfish to ask. "You go ahead."

Mitch and area law enforcement had a mixed relationship at best, not that I'd ever asked for details. He'd haunted the neighborhood my whole life, sometimes bumming change or a sandwich, sometimes joining me as I walked to school or work. Mitch was a local institution, a frequent write-in candidate for mayor. People liked him and his ever-changing signs. I liked him, too—his dentally challenged smile and easygoing attitude. As had Vaggio, who'd fed him on more nights than not.

I pulled my cell phone from my purse. The charge was low, but it connected. I speed-dialed 911, and crouched behind the prickly pear cacti dividing

Sanguini's parking lot from the one behind the Tex-Mex restaurant next door.

Despite ongoing farewells, Mitch lingered. Too loyal to bail. Tugging on the cuff of his flannel PJ bottoms, I urged him to hide beside me.

The police kept me on the line, answering questions, making it clear I was to vacate the area. I didn't.

I Vant to Suck Your Blood

They sent two squad cars, lights off, no sirens, one officer per sedan. Neither much older than me. I stayed still, waiting to see what would happen next.

Mitch hovered until they entered the building. "I'm going, gotta go, go."

"Go ahead," I whispered as Mitch began to creep away. "And by the way," I raised my voice, "good luck with the new sign."

He grinned, using it to wave good-bye, straightening to march to the sidewalk and plead his case to passersby.

Seconds later, the cops were escorting a skinny, cowpoke-looking guy out of the kitchen door to the back lot.

"Fellas, I'm telling you," he was saying in the kind of tone used to talk the suicidal off bridges, "I work here. A Mr. Davidson Morris hired me this morning. He gave me the keys, said we needed a new menu yesterday, and took off with his girlfriend to a concert in San Antonio. I thought I'd come in and get the feel of the place, start playing with the appliances . . ."

Oh, oh, oh no, I thought, relieved Vaggio's killer hadn't been lurking in Sanguini's kitchen, surprised Uncle D had neglected to tell me he'd finally managed to hire a chef, embarrassed I'd called the cops for nothing. None of which was an excuse for letting APD grill the guy or, worse, haul him away.

"Wait!" I called, bounding out of my hiding place, catching my leg on a cactus needle, drawing a thin line of blood. "Officers?"

The cuter of the two paused. "Stay back. This is police business."

"I'm Quincie Morris, the one who called 911. That man he just mentioned, Davidson Morris, is my uncle." Breathing hard, I slowed to a stop in front of them on the asphalt lot. "I'm sorry about the false alarm. I didn't know about Mr., uh, Mr. —"

"Johnson, Henry Johnson," the detainee pitched in.

After the police left, I gave my full attention to the new guy. His fair hair, widow's peak, gangly limbs, and western shirt. No more than twenty-two or three. I could hardly believe Uncle D had chosen such a young chef. We were desperate, but so much was at stake. It was a good thing my uncle had assigned me to keep an eye on him.

Johnson smiled, and I noticed the teeth. They were pointed, *all* of them.

"What the hell?" I asked.

"I almost forgot," Johnson replied with a horsey chuckle. "No wonder the coppers kept staring at me like that." He lifted out pointy wax teeth to reveal his real, regularly shaped lower set. "I was playing with these when the police showed up. What do you think?" He raised one bent elbow as if to cover all but his hazel eyes with an imaginary cape. "I vant to suck your blood."

"It's a little much," I said, laughing. "How's your cooking?"

"If you'd like to join me inside," he offered, "I'd be happy to show you."

I considered it, but I was still skittish about being in the kitchen and not quite ready yet to deal with Johnson one-on-one.

"Let's meet back here tomorrow morning," I said. "You, me, and my uncle D."

"Sounds swell," Johnson replied.

primo

FROM BLAH TO BITE

Uncle D shut the front door of the house behind us.

"Lock it," I urged.

"Oh, sure." As he reached into his pants pocket for the keys, his cell trilled.

I crossed my arms in the bright sunshine as my uncle took the call.

"Uh," he said into the phone. "Hang on." Uncle D put his hand over it and yawned. "It's Ruby. Can you give us a few minutes?"

Uncle D had shown up at home from his date with Ruby after 4 A.M. that morning, too mellowed on artificial substances to appreciate what I'd had to say about Johnson and my call to 911. A mere five hours later, his squinty, bloodshot eyes suggested he'd seen enough Death Jam for a while.

"We're going to be late," I said.

"Well, how 'bout this: you go ahead on foot. I'll take the car and beat you there. How does that sound?"

"Fine." I could only hope he and Ruby were in the midst of some kind of melodrama that would lead to a permanent breakup.

It's not like Uncle D had always been like this. He'd graduated with honors in poli sci from Texas State. But this past year he'd been more and more absent, wild. At work, he was usually his old self, but whatever. It was probably all Ruby's fault.

Making my way through the neighborhood, down the hill, up South Congress, I felt hyperaware of each passing stranger—a mom pushing a stroller of twins on the sidewalk, the neighborhood locals and tourists reading newspapers at the outdoor coffee shop, the gardening crew at the Unitarian church, the cops in the passing patrol car. I'd always paid attention when I walked, but not with this kind of intensity. Not as though anyone might be a killer.

I reminded myself that I couldn't let what happened to Vaggio change my whole life, that the street was busy, populated, and that at seventeen, I was practically a woman.

I let myself in the back door of Sanguini's, peeking into the kitchen first before stepping in. No Uncle D, and his convertible wasn't in the back lot yet either.

I heard a car pull in behind me and turned in the doorway to spot Johnson parking. He'd arrived at Sanguini's armed with an open box containing Calphalon cleaner, a tin of paprika, a small bottle of canola oil, and a collection of wooden forks, spoons, ladles, and spatulas. He was a few minutes early.

"Black cherry utensils," he said at the back step. "Very pathogen-resistant."

I wasn't sure whether to be impressed with his vigilance against salmonella or insulted by his implication about the cleanliness of Vaggio's kitchen. Then I remembered it had been last scrubbed by a private service recommended by APD's victim services counselor.

"Miss Morris?" Johnson asked.

The neighboring shops had opened minutes earlier. To the south, a few beat-up employee vehicles cluttered the lot next door. To the north, the lot was empty. On our property, one car had been parked between the lines in the first row, Johnson's beige SUV. I was being rude, not letting him in, but new hire or not, he was a stranger.

"I know what's wrong." Johnson handed me the box, plucking two spoons and holding them like a cross in front of his heart. "This is a 'vampire' restaurant. Aren't you going to say it?" His smile revealed classic fangs, which looked silly with his rodeo T-shirt and faded Wranglers. "Uh-hem."

"Huh?" I replied, no idea what he was talking about, trying to dredge up an inoffensive way to say I wasn't comfortable with the idea of the two of us alone together.

"Enter freely and of your own vill," he intoned. "Not," he went on conversationally, "that public places require an invitation, but just for fun."

And that was when Uncle D swung his yellow 1970 Cutlass convertible, also known as "The Banana," into the parking lot. Top down, in sorry need of a wash.

"Absolutely," I said. "Come on into the air conditioning." I called "Hey," to Uncle Davidson, whose returning wave looked weak. At least he was off the phone.

Turning on my sandal heel, I led the two men into what had been Vaggio's dream kitchen and dumped the box on the brushed stainless countertop, which was littered with more wooden kitchen utensils. Black cherry, no doubt, and crusty from food prep.

I peered into the stockpot filled with a watery mess of congealed rigatoni and the saucepan laden with rock-solid marinara. In addition to being disgusting, it spoke little of the new chef's creative zeal. To his credit, though, Johnson immediately picked up the pot and headed toward the sink to dump it out.

"Quincie, honey," Uncle D began. "You two can make nice while I go lie down in the break room. My head's killing—"

"No," I said. It was too soon for one of us to be in the break room while the other was in the kitchen with someone new. "I mean, why don't you two haul in the recliner?"

My uncle slung an arm around me, misunderstanding my anxiety as pissed-offness. "Sorry about last night."

With a sigh, I shrugged him off and fetched a bottle of orange Gatorade from the fridge. "Rehydrate," I suggested.

As Uncle Davidson and Johnson exited the stainless doors, I told myself they'd just be gone a minute and flipped the radio on to KUT. The piece playing was classical, Bach or Beethoven or one of those B-named composers.

I glanced from the door to the dining room to the door to the break room to the door to the hall to the door to the parking lot. When Uncle D had re-designed the place, he'd been thinking about flow, not defense.

But now we were taking precautions. Outside official business hours, the back door would always be locked. Uncle D had promised he'd remember. Plus, he was talking about hiring a couple of bouncers and/or security guards. Soon.

My uncle and Johnson returned with the old vinyl recliner, struggling to figure out the angle at the doorway. The beat-up chair looked out of place in the ultramodern kitchen, in front of the two cash registers. My uncle sank down and extended the footrest. The Gatorade bottle sat on the floor beside the chair, untouched as he closed his eyes. Meanwhile, Johnson got scrubbing and I pushed up on the counter to supervise.

By the time Johnson hung the saucepan onto the overhead rack, the radio was accompanied by the nasal snore of my uncle, who slept like the dead.

"Hungry?" the chef asked, lavender eyes attentive.

Wait a minute, I thought. "You have lavender eyes?"
They'd been—what?—hazel the night before.

"Contacts. I thought they might make me look more otherworldly."

"They do that," I agreed, taking inventory. Johnson wasn't classically handsome. His nose was too big, his smile too smug, his blond hair thinning on top. More skinny than slight. Cornball dimple in his left cheek. Bad dresser. Slouched. Pluses: youth; height, if he'd stand up straight; granny polite, though it came and went. Quirks: he wore two watches, expensive looking, that seemed out of place with the western clothes; his nails longer than usual for a man. And again, lavender eyes. "But they say more 'fairie prince' than 'vampire.'"

He retied his apron. "I'll try red next time, like in the movies."

I wasn't sure how much Uncle D had told Johnson, but it was my responsibility to get him up to speed. "You know," I said, "a lot of Sanguini's potential guests take the whole cape-and-incisors bit seriously."

"Cape?" he asked.

"Cape." Might as well spit it out, I decided. Uncle D envisioned the vampire chef not only as culinary expert but also as master of darkness. Each night's dinner climaxing in his leading a midnight toast. It was part of the job description. "His girlfriend, Ruby," I pointed at my snoozing guardian, "drinks human blood from virgin donors in Hill Country caves on nights with a full moon."

Johnson raised one eyebrow. "How do they know who's a virgin?"

"This isn't a joke!" I informed him. "We have to craft a complete gothic-inspired menu, *capisce*?" I held up a finger to stop him from interrupting. "And, at least so far as the general public is concerned, we also have to present you as reigning vampire king over anybody who dares to stroll through the front door."

"We?" Johnson asked, pulling a bag of tomatoes from a nearby bin. He'd apparently stocked it last night. "Look, Miss Morris, I understand you're a young woman. Very young, barely a woman, and you don't want to come off as a pushover. But you might reconsider your tone." He set the bag on the counter and grabbed a bowl from the cabinet. "You're lucky to have me. Nobody else even wanted this job because here at Sanguini's the first-year restaurant fatality rate does in fact mean *fatality* rate, and—"

"Hey!" I exclaimed, legs crossed in a manner hopefully more commanding than prissy. "A man died here, you know. Show a little respect."

"No worries, honey," my uncle piped up, having been awakened by our chatter. "I'll ask Ruby to give him a hand with his wardrobe and persona."

I remembered Ruby's laugh at Vaggio's funeral, the way she'd basked in the media limelight, how much time my uncle was spending with her already.

Not to be all territorial, but she wasn't the one whose grandparents and parents had once owned this restaurant. She wasn't the one who'd be taking it over one day. She wasn't even officially an employee. Besides, I'd thought *I* was in charge of the chef.

"Or," Uncle D mused, "maybe Ruby could play the master vampire and—"

"Wait!" I said, horrified at the idea of her in the spotlight night after night. "Let's not panic. I can help him. Really. *I'll* turn him into Count Sanguini."

"Not that Ruby doesn't seem like a great dame and all," Johnson said, reaching for a knife to dice, "but I'm sure Miss Morris and I can handle the job."

He didn't like Ruby either, I realized. Brownie points for him.

Waiting for my uncle's answer, I bit my lower lip. It was twenty-seven days until the relaunch. Engraved invitations for the Friday the 13th party had already been ordered and prepaid. Johnson had a menu to design. I had school, Kieren. It was a big job, an important job, way out of my area of expertise and smack in the middle of Ruby's. But I wanted to do it anyway, to put the finishing touch on Sanguini's, to create its star.

"All right, you two." Uncle D folded his hands, one atop another, like a corpse laid out for viewing. Then he pointed his toes as much as they would point in Birkenstocks. "If you run into trouble, just let me know."

THE MONSTER MAKER

*J*ohnson's rigatoni marinara was an orgasm in tomato sauce. If nothing else, the new chef could nail the basics.

After lunch, Uncle D took off to the restaurant supply store while I met with Johnson in the management office. It was bigger and cleaner than the old one we'd had before the remodel. My uncle had even sprung for a fake banana tree.

I took Uncle D's chair, and Johnson sat across from me. He'd brought an open bottle of blush wine, a '99 Sonoma Zinfandel from the fridge.

"It's too cold, even for a white," Johnson informed me, like he wasn't talking to a teenager, "and it's a day old, but we might as well finish it off."

I wasn't what anyone would call a partyer, but it wasn't like I'd never had a drink before either. Kieren and I snagged a couple of Coors every once in a great while, and there was that one disaster with the tequila. Besides, in my new assistant-manager-in-training mode, I didn't want to come off like a little kid. So I just nodded.

Johnson poured us each a glass, handed one to me, and raised his. "To Sanguini's."

How could I not drink to that? I raised my glass in reply, then brought it to my lips. The wine was chilly . . . and disturbing.

At my expression, Johnson laughed. "Something wrong?"

"Vaggio let me try wines sometimes," I said carefully. "I prefer white."

"Red is more sophisticated," Johnson replied. "Like you, sophisticated for your years but sure to improve with time."

I couldn't help being flattered and took another sip.

"Better?" he asked.

Not really, but I nodded again anyway.

"You'll develop a taste through continued exposure," Johnson explained. "You'll learn to appreciate its edge."

He sounded awfully sure about that, of himself. It was time to take charge of the situation. "Let's get your info in Frank," I said.

"Frank?" Johnson asked.

I grabbed it from inside the desk drawer. "My day planner."

"You *named* your day planner?"

"It's a Franklin Day Planner," I said. A leather-clad Christmas gift from Kieren, who knew me too well. "'Frank' is the natural diminutive."

"Like 'Frankenstein'?"

The monster maker, though this meeting was more about a make*over.*

Johnson was watching me, how I turned to the address pages, held my pen. It made me self-conscious about my scars.

As he rattled off an address, I copied it into Frank.

We'd have to start with the bio Uncle D wanted to adhere to the inside of the menu covers. A compelling identity for the vampire chef.

In real life, Henry Johnson hailed from Kansas City (Kansas City, Missouri; not Kansas City, Kansas), moved after graduating from high school to Paris (Paris, Texas; not Paris, France), attended the Southwest Culinary Arts Institute, and then worked one year as *sous*-chef and two as head chef at Chat Lunatique, also of Paris, Texas.

Johnson had just moved to Austin, he explained, when he came across Uncle D's help-wanted ad. "My last weekend in Paris was the same one my predecessor died. It's awkward, taking over under these circumstances. I'm sorry about your loss."

"Thanks," I replied. It was nice of him to say. Really, I appreciated it. But I couldn't talk about Vaggio right now without tearing up, and that wouldn't help anything. Uncle D had asked me to work with Johnson, and that's what I was going to do. Bio first. "About your stage name, do you have any suggestions?"

Johnson fidgeted in the chair across from the desk, too small for his frame. "How about 'Henry'?"

I rolled the wine on my tongue, trying to look neutral.

"'Hank'?" he asked.

"Welcome to the Million Bubba March."

"'Brad'?"

"Eh." It wasn't tragic.

He rubbed his chin. "How about 'Bradley Sanguini'?"

"'Bradley'?" I asked, raising my glass again.

"My mom's maiden name," he replied, brightening. "Or how about 'Brad, the Impaler'? As in 'Vlad,' like the Prince of Transylvania, except with—"

"'Bradley Sanguini' sounds fine."

"You know," Johnson said as I copied down the name, "we've been talking a lot about me, and I'm wondering. . . . Not to pry, but what're you doing at this joint? Shouldn't you be putting off your homework and looking for the ultimate zit cream and obsessing over who's taking you to the homecoming dance?"

"Lots of my classmates have afterschool and weekend jobs," I replied, hoping that he was referring to hypothetical zits. "This place means a lot to me, so I decided to do work-study in the afternoons, help out my uncle."

"Won't there be plenty of time for that later?" he asked.

I shrugged. "Who wants to be forever young? You can't do this, can't do that."

"So you don't have enough power?" Johnson asked. "Is that what you're saying?"

I fiddled with the zipper on Frank, embarrassed by the intensity of his attention.

"But adulthood," continued the barely twentysomething, "doesn't give you power over what matters most. It doesn't protect you from pain, loss, fate. That's part of being human."

Still . . . "I prefer to be in control."

"Isn't that about fear?" Johnson asked, swirling the liquid in his glass. "What are you so afraid . . . ?" Beats me what my face did, but he backed off. Quick. Far. Decisively. "I'm just trying to understand. Control of everyone? Everything?"

"I want to take care of myself, my own." That had been succinct. Adultlike. I was ready for a change of subject.

Johnson leaned forward. "Being the chef at your family's restaurant, would that make *me* your own?"

What a flirt! "An employee," I clarified. "Not a slave. Besides, my uncle runs the place, and he's more mellow than I am. Some free will is tolerated."

He laughed out loud at that, and I felt tension ease from my shoulders. The alcohol was helping with my stress level. A good call on the part of the new chef.

It wasn't his fault he wasn't Vaggio.

Johnson, no, that wouldn't do. From now on, I'd call him "Brad," short for "Bradley Sanguini." With my help, Brad would work out fine.

A knock sounded at the door.

As Brad reached for it, I said, "Wait," and then, louder, "Uncle Davidson?"

I thought he'd already left.

"Uh, it's Travis," a boy's voice sounded.

"And Clyde," another pitched in, brisker.

Kieren's friends. "How'd you get in?" I asked.

Clyde answered, "The back door was unlocked."

My stomach clenched as I wondered how Uncle D could forget.

Brad looked at me, and when I didn't object, he opened the door.

Standing before us were two guys, sophomores at my school.

Travis was maybe five foot four and stocky. He hopped back at my evaluating stare. Clyde stood a couple of inches shorter, his body slight. Each had a pronounced nose, though Clyde's came to a sharper point. Clyde also had black hair, going very early gray, *mucho* body hair on his arms and legs, and a smart-ass smile that showed too many tiny teeth. He broke the silence. "We're here to talk to your uncle about jobs."

Neither boy carried the kind of muscle that Kieren and his mama had inspired me to associate with Wolves, but I could always tell that neither Travis nor Clyde was a human being. I finished my glass, wishing Brad had brought back a full bottle.

SCHOOL AND OTHER SUCKY THINGS

I had every intention of walking to school. I'd resolved to do so every day after selling my temperamental Honda last May. It was a ten- to twelve-minute walk. No big deal. But then Monday morning came. It was already hot, and the rising sun made my eyes water. Fortunately, just as I'd walked out the door, Kieren pulled up curbside.

We hadn't talked about the possibility of his leaving for a pack since Saturday.

But I could feel it between us, crackling in the heat.

"You sure about this?" he asked, slowing his truck. "Working late, school in the morning. You're already dead on your feet."

My juggling work and school was nothing new. I yawned, shifting the seat belt.

Kieren took the hint. "Check it out," he said.

I opened my eyes to see Mitch at the corner. His sign read:

PRO-CHOICE AMISH
LAID-OFF TECH WORKER
NEEDS BOOZE & $

I lowered the window. "You're up early."

Mitch stepped into the street. "Miss Quincie! Hardly ever seen you before nine either. Not all summer anyway. Not since Mitch don't know when. Not since, shoot, hellfire, I, I sure am thirsty."

Digging into my purse, I slipped him a five.

"God bless, bless you. Gotta tell you, though. You gotta know. Cops talked to me, had lots of questions. So many. Too, too many. Asked about you and asked about you, too. I, I told 'em I didn't know nothing, not a thing, but that you was good kids."

Kieren and I exchanged a look.

"They're just doing their jobs," I told Mitch.

"Gotta go," Kieren pitched in. "Light." It'd just changed to green.

"Watch, watch. . . . Take good care, care for her," Mitch replied, backing away as traffic shifted into gear. "Bye-bye."

As we entered the intersection, Kieren said, "You don't think they suspect Mitch?"

"The cops? Why would they? It sounds like it's you and me that—"

"It's a high-profile case. There's a lot of pressure to get it solved, to bring in somebody and charge them. Mitch would make an easy scapegoat."

So would Kieren. Especially if it got out that he was part Wolf.

Kieren hadn't wanted to talk about his interview with APD, had dodged the question when I'd asked if the detective had demanded to know where he was born. But he did mention that werepeople and probably hybrids didn't have the same legal rights as humans. I studied his strong, brown hands on the steering wheel.

Moments later, Kieren pulled into the school parking lot and found a spot under a shade tree, several rows from the nearest car. Kieren shut off the engine and patted the dashboard, like the truck was Brazos.

Some kind of territory thing, I guessed. "I have to ask," he began. "Have you given any more thought to—"

"No." I reached over to turn the key so the air would come back on. I'd been able to tell from his tone where the conversation was headed.

"I'm asking you to talk to your uncle about making one adjustment. He can still retool the restaurant theme. Maybe the remodel is enough without the vampire crap."

I unbuckled my seat belt, reached for the door handle. "He's married to the idea," I snapped. "If Ruby loves it, he loves it."

"Quince—"

"God, can we just have a normal day?"

Kieren's touch was tentative on my forearm. "Normal sounds nice."

I knew my day would be lousy, though, when I saw the words "Bitch Sucks" spray-painted in red on my assigned locker. I could only hope the implication was sucking *blood*. Which, in itself . . . Christ.

Kieren was behind me, and I could feel him seethe.

Winnie Gerhard had bent over the nearest water fountain as an excuse to linger. Just great, I thought. The girl was the senior class equivalent of Fox News.

"I'm going to get a janitor," Kieren said.

"Wait, we've got class, and it's no big deal."
Nothing everyone hadn't seen or heard about already.

"I know. But you shouldn't have to look at it."

I nodded, raising my hand to spin the combination, put away my backpack. "I've got Econ first period."

"See you in English," he replied, marching off down the hall.

I watched him pass Quandra Perez—tall, dark, zowie, the kind of girl even straight girls lusted after—without so much as a glance. Kieren might not have ever acted on his feelings, but so far as I knew he'd always been loyal to me.

Quandra herself neared, casting a shocked look at my locker door, but she didn't say anything.

I used to have more friends, but in fifth grade, Sumi, my best friend who was a girl (as opposed to Kieren, my best friend who was a guy) had moved with her family back to India. A few cards, letters, then we lost touch. And the other girls, the ones from Sunday school and soccer. . . . They hadn't known what to say to me, how to act after my parents died. At the time, I'd felt deserted, angry because they seemed to think that being an orphan was somehow contagious. But then I'd had Vaggio, Kieren and his family, Uncle D. My life had seemed full enough between them and Fat Lorenzo's, and I'd lost interest in making new friends.

Tears pricked my eyes as I realized that soon it would just be me and my uncle.

And, of course, Sanguini's.

The bell rang, and I was alone in the hallway.

"Miss Morris," a man's voice called as heavy footsteps hit industrial tile.

I shut my locker door, Econ text and Frank in hand, before turning to face Vice Principal "Hardass" Harding. "Sorry I'm running late," I said. "I had a problem with my locker this morning."

"About that. Why don't you follow me?"

I could pick up Econ notes later. Resigned, I took a few seconds to open my locker again, shove my text into it, and shut the door harder than necessary. Then, hugging Frank to my chest, I followed the vice principal to his office, figuring he wanted to quiz me on likely locker vandals. Not that I had lead one.

It was a drag having to go through the motions, but I didn't have much choice. Not with Harding on the case. He was really something. Freshmen whispered of foster-care kids who got hauled into his office and were never seen again. Even varsity defensive linemen were all "yes, sir," "no, sir," "whatever you say, sir" to the VP.

Personally, I thought Harding got off on it, his hard-ass rep, which at least would explain the medieval ax hanging on the wall of his otherwise blah administrative office.

Rounding his desk to sit across from me, he began, "Now, Miss Morris, everyone here is sympathetic to your unusual circumstances."

Uh-huh.

"I took the liberty of reviewing your records this morning, and I noticed that you've elected to go half days and take work-study credit."

Uh-huh.

"Given your need to recover and this morning's unfortunate incident, I thought you might prefer to complete your requirements for graduation via a homeschool arrangement."

What? I blinked. Half days were one thing, but this would mean good-bye to school as of immediately.

"Your uncle . . . I thought the two of you might be able to work out an acceptable academic regimen. Took the liberty of calling him just before you arrived, and he seemed open to my suggestion."

Really? I thought, baffled. "I can handle classes," I said. "I'm a good student." Not top-ten like Kieren, but honor roll.

"Think it over," Harding replied, glancing at his ax. "Talk to your uncle. Let me know when you change your mind."

FANG SHUI

*I*t should've felt like work, not a date. I blamed the atmosphere, the fang shui. Brad had gone so far as to dim the overheads and turn on both the tiny candle-style lamp on my table as well as the wall sconce above the booth. He'd also activated the sound system, playing instrumental jazz. He'd even opened a bottle of Cabernet.

"How was your morning?" Brad asked, ladling minestrone into my bowl. "Pencils, books, dirty looks?"

"Typical first day song and dance." After school, I used to taste-test for Vaggio and clue him in on my latest news. But I didn't know Brad well enough to confide.

"And do you have a sweetheart there? A puppy love?"

Suddenly, I lost my appetite.

"You don't like it?" Gesturing to the soup, Brad slid into the black leather bench opposite mine. "How can you not like it? You haven't even tasted it yet."

I slipped the crimson napkin to my overalls lap, grateful to be focusing on food rather than my personal life. "It's minestrone."

Brad met my eyes, raised a questioning brow. He'd put in the red contacts, as promised. They looked good with the fangs, which he'd persisted in wearing. He'd also traded in his 'kicker apparel for a solid royal blue oxford and khakis. Brown leather belt, brown leather shoes, brown leather watchbands. The kind of vampire a nice girl could bring home to her parents, if she had parents.

Mama and Daddy had been Kieren's godparents, I recalled. They adored him. Daddy used to tease that we'd get married one day.

Focus, I thought. *Food.* As Vaggio had often pointed out, many a dive did booming business because the food was to die for. Sanguini's could settle for no less.

I dipped my spoon into the bowl, opened my mouth, and . . . good. The minestrone? Scrumptious, savory heaven. Hot enough to scintillate without scorching, taut onions, sinful bacon bits, chopped celery, fresh spaghetti, plump red beans, a touch of kale . . .

"Well done," I said. "Or not well done. But . . . Well. Done. And, bonus, Italian." I tried another spoonful. *Blessed Mother of Minestrone*. I took the moment to stir. "But Pasta Perfecto serves minestrone. So does The Olive Garden. The people at Campbell's sell it in a can."

"But my minestrone is better—"

"So was Vaggio's," I replied, swallowing hard, "and we still lost out to the competition." I flipped to a blank page in Frank, which lay open on the table, and picked up my pen. "What else are you thinking for the menu?"

One of Brad's loafers nudged my right foot, and I moved it back. "We need a soup, I think. I also make a good chowder, by the way. Or there's a stew, a mushroom stew I could try for an entrée." Brad reached for the wine bottle and filled my glass.

"I'll just have water," I said.

"The guests will be having the dishes with wine," he countered.

That made sense, I guessed, trying it. This glass tasted better than the one I'd had the other day. I supposed I preferred the Cab to the Zin. It also somehow made a terrible day seem instantly not so bad

"Despite the bones," Brad went on, "Texas quail could be interesting. For now, I've got a corn conchiglie salad and tiramisù, which you'll have to excuse me to—"

"Hang on. Vampires, remember?" Either Brad didn't get the concept of crawly creepies or he was suffering from a mental block. I gave the room another perusal. It could've been any high-end restaurant dining area. It was the suggestion of the vampire that heightened its intrigue. "I'm not complaining about the quality of your cooking, but atmosphere alone isn't going to cut it. We need to submerge people, even with the menu, like—"

"A scary movie?"

I dabbed my lips with my napkin, tried the wine again. "More expensive. And interactive, like—"

"A ritzy tourist trap?"

"Ritzy role-playing game," I replied. "Sanguini's is providing the menu and venue, but the guests will be participants, not passive audience members." I shifted in the booth, and my foot grazed his ankle that time. Accidentally. "You need to create some sense of drama, I guess. Take it up a notch or three."

"I did do some research for this job," Brad countered, "and your idea of vampires seems pretty stereotypical for—"

"It's what the guests will expect," I replied.

Something banged in the kitchen, and I flinched.

"Easy," Brad soothed. "That's your uncle and Ruby." He lowered his voice. "Davidson seems swell, but what you said the other day about her—"

The stainless kitchen door swung open, and, as if on cue, Ruby sashayed across the midnight blue carpet. Today's ensemble was a shiny black leather bodysuit with spaghetti straps over a long-sleeve, black lace shirt, with ankle-high shoes, lace-up, and a black velvet ribbon fastened at the collarbone. Her trademark scent preceded her, a cinnamon musk. "Hello, kids," she began, clapping once like a less-than-thrilled theater fan. "My, isn't this cozy. Quincie, Quincie, Quincie, I thought you already had a boyfriend."

"We're working," I put in. "Working on the menu."

I didn't get what they saw in each other, my uncle and Ruby. Flower Child meets Child of the Night and all that. Their twisted world of black daisies, bloody peace signs, and fang-dipped smiley faces. Not something to dwell on, but the sex must've been spectacular.

"Hate to say so," Ruby replied, hovering over the booth, outlined lips at full pout, "but Sanguini's 'vampire chef' could double as a JCPenney model." She made a show of considering. "The clothes, anyway."

The average blind man saw more beauty in a day than Ruby did in a lifetime. Maybe that was my uncle's attraction to her. The yin-yang. Her darkness, his light.

"Go away," I said, giving up on politeness.

"I'm just saying," Ruby went on, "he could be the death of this operation."

She was rooting for Brad's makeover to bomb, I realized. Uncle D must've talked to her about playing master vampire, and—big surprise—she'd loved the idea.

Too bad. Brad had already agreed to go shopping with me the next day.

"Ruby," Uncle Davidson called, sticking his head in the room, "let's let these two get to know each other." It was like he was the set-up guy, hustling her away from our blind date. And there was that word again. "Date."

Ruby licked her lips as though she could read my mind, and before I knew it, bent to kiss me, kiss *me* on the lips. Warm, wet, smiling. Pulling back, her up-turned green eyes peered into mine.

It was possible, I thought, that in time I might grow to hate her.

Good kisser, though.

"You should learn to listen," Ruby suggested, sashaying away. "Ta."

Uncle Davidson called "See ya," apparently with-out having noticed my drinking, and for a while, Brad and I let the jazz take over the room. I finished my soup. He poured himself a glass of wine. The quiet was clunky.

"Thing about Ruby," I said, "she seems to think being cryptic is some kind of substitute for having a decent personality."

"The living vampirism," he began, "how—"

"Don't let her get to you," I said. "Sanguini's is li-able to get a lot worse waltzing through the front door." Better the front door than the back, I thought, wondering if this time Uncle D had remembered to lock behind them.

"I'm not worried," Brad assured me.

But I was. It had been only ten days since Vaggio's murder. No arrests.

I took a deep, cleansing breath, finished my glass.

"However," Brad went on. "I've had a pair of brothers, both hard-boiled sorts, working on my house—refinishing the floors, replacing broken windows, and so forth. They mentioned needing extra cash. Do you think I'd be overstepping bounds if I suggested them to your uncle for the bouncer jobs?"

"No!" I took a breath. "I mean, no, I'm sure he'd appreciate that."

"Done. I should get to the kitchen to finish your conchiglie salad," Brad added, rising from the booth, taking my bowl with him. "That is if you're still hungry?"

I paused, realizing he'd caught me licking my soupspoon.

"More giggle water?" he asked, lifting the bottle of wine.

ALL THE WORLD'S A STAGE

*T*he following morning I knocked on Uncle D's bedroom door until he got up.

"I'll just have coffee," he said, yawning in cutoff sweatpants and a sleeveless T.

While he fetched himself a cup, I heated a breakfast taco in the microwave, poured myself a glass of orange juice, and then joined Uncle D at the table. "Why did you tell the vice principal I would do homeschool?"

I hadn't wanted to bring it up at the restaurant with Ruby and Brad around, but it had freaked me out that he'd agree to such a thing without our even talking about it first.

"Good morning to you, too," he replied, adding sugar to his "World's Greatest Uncle" mug. "Honey, you know how much I need you at work, and it's not like you have a lot of friends at school, compared to at the restaurant. Oh, speaking of which, Sergio's coming back, did I tell you? He was thrilled to quit that job at—"

"I have Kieren," I said, taking a bite of my taco.

Looking unimpressed, Uncle D shifted gears on me. "What do you think of our chef? Not bad, eh? And he can cook, too."

Before he could stray further off base, I said, "No homeschool, okay? I'm happy with going mornings, and anyway, Brad told me he hadn't gotten to work before noon or so these past couple of days." I couldn't imagine Uncle D cared that much, but if need be, I was willing to take a stand. I wanted to help out at Sanguini's, and I would, but lusting after Kieren in English class was the highlight of my day.

"Excuse me for being considerate." Uncle D lifted his coffee to sip, set it down quickly, and smacked his lips. "Hot, hot, hot. But as I was saying, about 'Brad,' as you two have decided to call him. . . . I like that, by the way. What do you think?"

"He's got potential," I said. "By the time I'm done with him—"

"Good," Uncle D informed me. "When I interviewed him, I told him how special you were, how much Sanguini's is in your blood. I don't know if he totally believed me then, but now—"

The phone rang, and I jumped for it.

Kieren opened with, "Why didn't you call me back last night?"

"You called?" I'd been stressed, thinking he hadn't. We usually talked a few times a day, but he was so moody lately.

"I left a message with your uncle."

Huh. "Sorry, I didn't get it."

"You could've called when you got home," Kieren said. "Or e-mailed." He'd had his cell permanently confiscated months ago when his mama caught us talking after midnight. Harsh, but it hadn't been the first time—that had been during the first week of finals, and he'd been warned more than once.

I took a breath. "It was late and I was tired and—"

"I was worried. I stayed up all night wondering—"

"I'm sorry, but I was working and—"

"With the new chef?" he wanted to know.

I wasn't loving Kieren's tone of voice. "I don't think you understand how important it is that—"

"Fine."

"Fine," I replied.

We hung up, and I sat down at the table with my uncle, who was staring at his coffee like it held the secrets to the universe. "I'm sorry that I forgot to tell you the boy called. I thought I wrote it down somewhere. I don't know where my brain is."

I did. Between raising me, managing the restaurant relaunch, losing Vaggio, falling in lust with Ruby . . . I sipped my juice. "Kieren's just a little edgy these days."

"Do you think that's something I should mention to the police?"

The question caught me by surprise. "What do you mean?"

"The detective said to call back if anything seemed unusual."

Even though he hadn't been at the scene, Uncle D was questioned the day after the murder. I thought about it. Had Daddy ever confided to Uncle D about Kieren's Wolf heritage? That possibility, coupled with the circumstances of Vaggio's murder, made me wonder. What might Uncle D have told the police?

*　　*　　*

After school, I was back on the job. Dragged Brad out of the Sanguini's kitchen and down the sidewalk to All the World's a Stage. The clerk helped us pull various male vampire costumes, and we sorted through them to find the most promising.

"I've already got the eyes and fangs," Brad said. "Do I need a whole outfit?"

I held up a full-length blue suede western jacket, shook my head, and hung it on a spare rack. "People are going to be coming in from all over hell and half of Texas," I said. "We need to give them a show."

Brad held a silky white shirt up to himself. "White washes me out, I think."

I smirked. "Go look at it in a mirror."

"If we find something worth trying on," he said, "I'll look."

Brad had sounded about as hopeful as I felt.

"You're really tall," I said. "Slender, too." More attractive than I'd thought at first glance. It was the kind of face that grew on you. Not so obviously handsome like Kieren's, so obviously masculine. But sophisticated, like his affection for wine.

Our best candidate: a black-and-crimson suit, unlined, shirt sewn into the pants, buttons made of plastic. A black-and-red plastic medallion hung from a frayed black ribbon. Brad claimed to already have black dress shoes, but . . .

"Too chintzy," he said.

"Too chintzy," I agreed. "And too short in the arms and legs."

MOON LITE

*T*wo days later, Brad's never-ending quest for a menacing menu, well, never ended. While my fellow seniors, the ones with a parent or three, busied themselves with Back to School Night, I broke the news: "The most gothic thing about your eggplant parmesan is the fact that a purple vegetable exists in nature."

"I need a vegetarian selection," he replied, rinsing a long, wooden spoon.

Travis, who was doing dishes, stayed out of it. My uncle had scheduled him and Clyde on alternate days until the debut party. Travis was sweeter, easy to work with. The more Brad and I bantered, the more Travis seemed to want to take cover inside the sink.

Brad, on the other hand, rejoiced in it. He loved to cook, loved to talk cooking. Like Kieren loved his werestudies. Like Vaggio had loved good women. Like Uncle D loved bad women. Like Daddy had loved ancient cultures and Mama had loved Fat Lorenzo's. Brad gobbled it up. He was starting to seem almost as committed to Sanguini's as I was.

"It's after midnight," I said, as he poured more Chianti into the wine glass I'd left on the butcher's block.

I kept waiting for Uncle D to say something about Brad drinking on the job, about Brad drinking on the job with me. Not with his taste in recreational substances that he had much room to talk. But *nada*. It was as though Uncle D had woken up one morning and saw me in a new, more grown-up light. I liked it.

"How about a ride home?" Brad asked.

"I'm taking The Banana."

"About that . . ." Brad peered over Travis's shoulder to check progress. "Ruby and Davidson picked up the car a few hours ago, while you were rearranging the sample wait station for the thousandth time. I meant to mention it."

"I guess he's feeling better," I muttered. That morning Uncle D had said he was too sick to come in. Excusing myself to duck into the break room, I used my dying cell phone to call him—no answer.

I could've tried Kieren, but it was late, a school night. I'd just wake up everybody. Meghan was in bed by eight or so. Meara and Roberto after the late news.

Besides, since our blowup on the phone, things had been even more strained between me and Kieren. At school, we'd both pretended like nothing had happened, just like we pretended he wasn't leaving and we pretended he didn't blame Sanguini's for Vaggio's death. It was becoming harder and harder to talk at all.

"Well?" Brad asked when I returned to the kitchen. We'd mostly cleaned up, but he was still wiping down the stovetop.

"My uncle's not answering," I said, frustrated. It would be better once the restaurant opened and he got back on a regular schedule, working days and nights.

"I'd be honored to escort you home, Miss Morris." Brad checked his two wristwatches, offered an inviting smile. "No trouble. "

What was happening here? I wondered. It was like Brad and I were developing some kind of vibe. Not that anything would come of it. I already had Kieren, or at least, I hadn't given up yet on wanting to have Kieren, and besides, the way Brad kept tasting the food and spitting it out in the trash—kind of a turnoff.

Now, Kieren knew how to devour . . . I shoved the thought away.

Brad was who mattered at the moment. Sanguini's success depended on its chef. I wasn't sure how else I'd get home, but I didn't want to lead him on either.

"Now, then," Brad added, tossing his paper towel in the trash. "I know you're invested in being an obsessive-compulsive over-the-top risk taker. Which, I must say, makes you a contradictory personality type. And a fascinating one at that. But think before you turn me down."

Mildly O-C maybe, but . . . "I am not an over-the-top risk—"

"In addition to that hirsute boy your uncle doesn't approve of," Brad argued, "and your being in the restaurant business, I'm thinking that walking home alone is foolhardy. You can't control what happens in the night, Miss Morris."

It was annoying that he and Uncle D had been talking about my personal life. I patted Brad's shoulder, a nonflirtatious pat. "Save it for the clientele. I'm wiped, and Travis isn't done. Besides, I've walked home from work tons of times." Not at night, though. Not really. I took a gulp of Chianti. "Odds are—"

"Odds don't matter when a predator beats them," Brad replied. "That's the game some beasts live for, beasts that should've been hunted to extinction long, long ago."

I bristled. "If you're talking about werepeople—"

"Translating to 'man-people'— of all the PC nonsense." Brad's voice gentled. "I know you've been avoiding the media, but in the past month, Bear tracks were found outside the window of a missing toddler in Salt Lake City. A Cat shredded a stripper in New Jersey to ribbons. Russian authorities identified a terror cell of werehyenas—"

"I get it." Enough already, I thought. No way was he taking me home now.

"They aren't people," Brad added. "They are not and have never been human beings. It's that form, Miss Morris, the familiar form, that's the disguise. The scam. They're monsters in masquerade. Pretending to be people—neighbors, friends, lovers even. Using their humanlike skins to deceive."

"And you're the expert?" I asked, trying not to overreact. Most humans had issues with shifters. I'd seen a poll on TV not long ago that said something like 80 percent of humans thought of werepeople as dangerous and more than half considered them somehow demonic. Even Uncle D had been known to make the occasional remark. But that didn't make it any less racist or species-ist or something-ist.

"Think of your friend Vaggio," Brad said. "What one of them did to him."

"I'm out of here," I replied. "Kill the lights, will you?"

Brad smiled in apparent surrender. "I will."

"Deadbolt the front door behind me?" I'd been avoiding the parking lot after dark.

"That, too."

I picked up my glass and held it against my forehead, trying to ease the ache. I couldn't just brush off Brad. He meant well, and he was on the home team now. Setting my glass back down, I said, "You can call me 'Quincie.'"

Brad reached for my scarred hand. "Be careful, Quincie."

I looked at where our skin met. Then I left, crossing through the dining room to the foyer, stepping onto the busy sidewalk.

"Hey, Quincie!" Travis called, just as I'd passed the vacant lot next door, lumbering to catch up with a paper bag in his thick hands. "You forgot this." It was the care package that Brad had whipped together for Uncle Davidson.

"Thanks," I said. "And thanks for staying late."

"Leavin' now," Travis replied with a shrug. "I told my mom I'd be home by a half-hour ago, and Brad said he'd finish the dishes."

I waved, and Travis motored in the opposite direction.

At twelve thirtyish on a Thursday night—make that Friday morning—the weekend was already in full swing. Music aficionados congregated outside the clubs, tourists stumbled out of margarita bars, and the shops had been closed tight. The Capitol Motel, the Spanish-style motel, and the '50s-retro one next door to it all posted No Vacancy. The sky was murky, like it had been covered by a smoky blanket. It had rained earlier that evening, and the asphalt felt slick in places.

Stumbling on the curb, I nearly dropped my uncle's chicken soup. Watching where I was going couldn't hurt. The sporadic traffic to my right, storefront windows to my left. Dull security lights, crisp neon.

What was I thinking, I wondered steps later, walking by myself at this hour? I hated to admit it, but Brad had a point. He was just so hard to read, and then he'd hit too close to home. Reminded me of what I was trying to forget. The investigation. Kieren as a possible suspect. A murderer on the loose. Brad seemed to think I was in some kind of denial, and if that was true, so be it. Denial had been keeping me functional. It was working for me. Or at least it had been.

I paused, considering. Brad would never hear me knocking at the front door, and it seemed safer to stay on the sidewalk with the crowd than go around the building by myself. Besides, I hated the thought of crawling back.

Passing a couple of bikers (the kind that wore leather, not the kind that won the Tour de France), I told myself I was worrying for *nada,* but I felt watched.

I squinted, scanning the flyers stapled to a pole. Among those announcing "roommates wanted," an anti-death-penalty rally, and a band called The Screaming Head Colds, were others with black-and-white photos of missing people and pets.

At the next intersection, I glanced behind me and spotted a male figure, half obscured by a giant yucca, advancing fast. Was he after me, I wondered, or just trying to make last call? There hadn't been another murder since Vaggio's, and that had been not quite two weeks earlier. But damn, why hadn't I waited for Brad to give me a ride?

Maybe the drinking had impaired my judgment.

My keys extended from between each of the fingers on my right hand. My house waited another block away. I glanced back, but a laughing group of partyers had spilled onto the sidewalk between me and my would-be pursuer.

Setting the bag beside a row of newspaper dispensers, I decided, tipsy or no, to make a run for it. If my uncle could go out with his girlfriend, he could live without his soup, and carrying it would slow me down.

I passed a petite woman in blond pigtails, lugging a guitar case. A guy with green hair, wearing chains on his wrists and as a belt.

The sidewalk was uneven, downhill to the stoplight. Then I turned left, hoping whoever it was hadn't seen me as I continued up, *up* at a steep incline. A canopy of trees, sleeping houses lay ahead.

A few steps more, one right turn, I'd be on my own street. But . . .

The hill.

Fatigue.

Wine.

I didn't get twenty feet before I heard footsteps closing in. Panting. Something grazed the small of my back.

"Qu—"

I turned to strike back—to hit, kick, bite, if I

could sink my teeth into anything. Knowing I'd never outrun him. My fist tightened around my key chain, and I aimed for an eye. Swinging too hard, I missed, throwing my whole body off balance. His, too. Our legs tangled, and we collapsed in a heap on the damp sidewalk. My teeth cut my tongue on impact. Pain surged up my limbs, my side.

"Qu-Quince!"

Kieren? I scrambled away from him.

"Quince?" he said.

I didn't move, couldn't.

"You're not afraid of *me*, are you?"

"No," I breathed. "Don't be ridiculous." My heart was pounding double time, and Kieren was lucky I hadn't stabbed one of his pretty brown eyes out. I'd hurt my hip, elbow, forearm. The injuries stung in some places, ached in others. Nothing broken, but the gravel had done a number on my skin. "What are you doing?"

He climbed to his feet, offered me a hand up. "I was trying to —"

"What? Scare the bejeezus out of me?"

"Catch up. Travis called me at Clyde's, said you were walking home alone, so I took off as fast as I could and . . ."

Here he was. We stood together in the darkness. In my neighborhood, steps from the turnoff onto my dead-end street. No streetlight. No moonlight tower. No moon.

"Your folks let you stay out this late on a Thursday?" I asked.

"We're seniors now," Kieren said, brushing dirt from my jeans and T-shirt.

And, I remembered with a pang, the Moraleses were already planning on him going out on his own soon anyway.

"You never walk alone at night," Kieren added.

"I know." His touch felt good. My anger melted as I ached for more of it.

We limped together down the middle of the street, up the walk to my house.

I'd overreacted, I realized. Too much pressure, adrenaline.

Glancing over my shoulder, I unlocked the front door. "My uncle's out with Ruby." I crossed the threshold, flipped on the porch light. Kieren's wild hair looked fuller, more lush. Since this morning, he'd grown a goatee. Tight T-shirt, button-fly jeans, black boots. Mussy, furry, and yummy delicious. "Wanna come in?" I asked.

Something flashed in his eyes. Temptation, heat, hunger. Pack or no pack, had I finally worn him down? Then his expression grew concerned.

"You've been drinking," he said.

I leaned against the doorframe. "That's not why I'm inviting you in."

I sensed victory as Kieren took a step forward, but when I moved aside to let him pass, I heard Uncle D's voice from the family room.

"It's a school night, honey."

When did he get home?

HOME WORK

$\mathcal{U}$ncle D had gone with me to church downtown, followed by a gospel brunch in New Braunfels. A just-us day, something we used to do more often.

That afternoon, he lounged on the sofa, reading the latest coverage of Vaggio's murder. Another article that didn't say anything new. Uncle D had offered a reward for info, but so far, no luck. He shuffled the paper, turning to regional news. "Looks like that little girl who went missing in the Woodlands died in a weregator attack."

I didn't reply. According to Kieren, though, Gators were an urban myth started by New Orleans swamp tour guides. Not that I hadn't given up on fairness in reporting long ago, at least when it came to stories about shifters. The lynching of werepeople, for example, or cross burnings on their front yards never even made the news unless there were photos, video. Even then, it was too often implied the victims might've somehow provoked the attack.

At my apparent disinterest, Uncle D changed the subject. "Need any help?"

Sitting cross-legged on the floor, I looked up from the book opened on the coffee table. "I've got this reading assignment for chem and—"

"Chem." Uncle D folded the paper and sat up. "How about a . . . I guess we don't have much in the fridge. I haven't had a chance to go grocery shopping. Maybe something to drink?" He leaned forward. "Speaking of which, I noticed that you've become quite the red wine drinker." As I was bracing to defend myself, Uncle D added, "I brought home a bottle of the house Chianti, if you're interested."

Wow, I thought. Letting my drinking slide was one thing, but actually offering me booze. . . . Apparently Kieren's folks weren't the only adults who thought high school seniors deserved to be treated more like grown-ups. "No thanks," I said, tempted. "I need to concentrate." I shot him a sideways glance. "You didn't take chem as your lab science at Texas State?"

He shook his head. "Geography."

"Maps?"

He laughed. "Landforms, ocean currents, clouds . . ."

"Wimp," I replied.

It was nice, having a regular day. I'd felt so maxed out lately. In the past year or so, though, Uncle D had stopped busting on me about my homework and housework, despite my sliding grades and the fuzzy black ick growing on the shower curtain. But today, here I was, doing chem and—I wrinkled my nose—resolving to toss the shower curtain in the washing machine.

I didn't want to think about danger or death, especially now, but at least I could tell Kieren I'd tried. "So, um, master scientist, I was wondering. Brad's such an amazing chef, and the restaurant looks better than ever. It seems like the only thing that's not coming together is the, uh, vampire angle."

"Don't you like it?" my uncle asked, standing. "I thought you liked it."

Oh, man. I didn't know what kind of response I'd expected, but Uncle D looked wounded. No way could I bring up Kieren's theory about Sanguini's attracting a killer vampire, I realized. Uncle D would freak. "I like it," I said. "I *do*. But some people—"

"What people?" he asked, sounding suspicious.

I set my chem book on my neglected English journal, unsure of what to say.

Uncle D studied me for a long moment before going to the kitchen to fetch each of us a glass of Chianti. "To family," he said, and we clinked, drank. "Friends come and go, but family is forever."

Not exactly subtle, my uncle. So he didn't love Kieren. What else was new? But he had reminded me of something else I wanted to bring up. If Uncle D was entitled to his opinion, then so was I. "Speaking of friends, I know you're into Ruby but, I, um . . ."

Uncle D swallowed more wine and confided, blowing my entire train of thought, "Ruby has been searching for a real vampire."

I couldn't help being fascinated, horrified. "How? Online?"

This time he was the one who didn't answer, and I could've kicked myself. Despite his casual tone, I was starting to believe Uncle D really loved her. He must have been mortified, I realized. Ruby's obsession was spiraling out of control.

"You think she wants to go all the way?" I asked, sipping my drink.

"She talks about it a lot. Vampire this, vampire that." He paused, setting aside his glass. "It's not that I don't understand. Think of all those people. The ones who watch vampire movies, read vampire novels, the ones so eager to dine at Sanguini's. Who called the first day we started taking reservations. They're lured by the sensuality, the idea of eternal youth." His lips quirked. "There are those who'd say it's cheaper than Botox, and the effects are permanent."

I recognized most of the spiel from promotional interviews he'd done for Sanguini's. The way Uncle D spun it, vampirism sounded like undead party time. But what Ruby was talking about, the real deal—it was worse than suicide. It was one thing to playact at being a monster. It was another to give up your life, your immortal soul.

Something occurred to me. "You don't think she's already . . . ?"

"Nah. I'm sleeping with her. Believe me, she's a lot more alive than I am."

Ew, I thought. "And that's the appeal?" I asked, appreciating that they always did it at her place. "The sex?"

"It's . . . she's easy." At my expression, he added, "Not like that. Or, not *just* like that. Ruby wanted me from the start, no games. It seems like it's been a long time since everything hasn't been harder than it should be. Women included."

I thought back to the reception at Fat Lorenzo's after my parents' funeral, overhearing Uncle D's high school and college buddies talk about how unfair it was that he'd have to give up his youth to take care of the restaurant, of me. They'd all faded away not long afterward. He had to get lonely. A teenage niece could only provide so much company, and Daddy had been his best friend. Now with Vaggio gone, too . . .

"Let's take a walk," I suggested, "go shopping on South Congress." I tilted my head at him. "I could use a new pair of cowboy boots. Something red in honor of Sanguini's. And I know just the uncle to buy them for me."

Metamorphoses

Mrs. Levy strolled through the aisles of second period English, handing back journals with red pluses or minuses on them. That Thursday, mine had a minus.

"How are you, Quincie?" she asked, pausing at my desk.

It was back, The Tone. The one I'd heard so often after my folks died, this time because of Vaggio. Despite the locker incident, my classmates were treating me like usual, which was to say like furniture. But a couple of my teachers had been using The Tone, especially since my grades had started to slip. It was almost enough to make me reconsider homeschooling. I tried to look perky. "Fine, thanks."

She put down Kieren's journal on the desk next to mine. A plus. I could imagine him, sprawled, disheveled, on his water bed, scribbling away. Mmmm . . . nice.

When Mrs. Levy moved on, I whispered, "Kiss ass."

Kieren put his forefinger over his lips to say "Hush."

I smirked back. I always did crappy in classes I had with Kieren, but he was so gorgeous. I couldn't help myself. He *was* one of the good guys, I thought.

Mrs. Levy took her place at the front of the room and turned hopeful eyes on her flock. "Who can tell me about one of the many retellings of Ovid's *Metamorphoses*?"

Tamika Thomas's and Angela Gray's hands shot up like it was a synchronized sport, but Mrs. Levy ignored them to call on Ricardo Bentley, linebacker. Due to grades, he was in danger of having to sit out this weekend's football game, and our teacher was enough of a fan to give him a shot at improving his participation marks.

Most of the class, including Kieren, cared enough

to wait rapt for Ricardo's response. I took advantage of the shift in attention to indulge in my favorite pastime: drooling over my best friend. He had the longest, blackest eyelashes and the fullest lips. When he licked the bottom one, I squirmed in the institutional plastic chair.

As Ricardo wowed the masses with his analysis of why *Pretty Woman* was more on point than *She's All That,* my gaze slid to Kieren's hands. One resting on the desk, one curled around a blue-ink pen. Imagined them in my hair, sweeping it aside as he leaned in to nibble my shoulder. Imagined them falling lower, caressing my spine before sliding farther down. Imagined them taking mine, drawing me to lie beside him. Remembered the closest I'd gotten, our hands intertwined. At Vaggio's memorial on Mount Bonnell. In the back seat of the police car, his stained with Vaggio's blood. At the railroad bridge, his stained with mine. Straining into claws. Piercing. Tearing.

"Quincie?" Mrs. Levy called. "Are you with us this morning?"

After school, I paced as Brad tried on a red satin shirt and black leather pants in the dressing room at Babes & Bikes on Sixth Street.

"You've been out of sorts lately," Brad observed from behind the curtain. "Your uncle is worried about you. He thinks it has something to do with your boyfriend."

"I don't have a boyfriend," I said. "I have a boy who's a friend. Or, at least I do for now. He's . . . moving away."

"Let me guess," the chef replied. "Out-of-state college?"

"Something like that." I couldn't help wondering if it was easier to fixate on Kieren's joining a Wolf pack than whether he might *have* lost control with Vaggio. No matter how hard I tried, I couldn't get it out of my head. If Kieren hadn't told me the whole truth about the pack, maybe he hadn't told me the whole truth about that night, too. Miz Morales had seemed so convinced his leaving was the only way. Maybe it was her he'd talked to. If I still had a mama, that's who I'd go to now.

God, what was wrong with me? Why didn't I know anything? One minute I wanted to jump Kieren and the next I wanted to run away from him and hide. One minute I thought we should be together forever and the next I just wanted him to go ahead and get the hell out of my life.

I paced faster, turning without paying attention, knocking into a display of chain belts and wrist cuffs, causing it to topple over with a jangling crash.

"Quincie!" Brad exclaimed from the dressing room.

"Nothing's broken," I said, scrambling to restore order. "I'm just a complete spaz."

"If it makes you feel any better," Brad said, "I'm not going anywhere."

Actually, it did. With things so uncertain between me and Kieren, Uncle D always off with Ruby or busy working, and Vaggio dead, it was nice to have someone new to talk to. I didn't even mind Brad's flirting. It seemed harmless enough, I thought, putting the last of the belts back on their hooks, and Kieren never flirted. He was so earnest, so careful around me. Brad made me feel like I was a girl somebody could really want.

"Here goes," Brad said, stepping out into the shop. He struck a pose, showing off the black leather and red satin. "Too slutty?"

Wow. "Oh, yeah."

No Rest for the Wicked

*B*rad glided through the dining room doorway. Black tux, white shirt, black dress shoes, white calla lily boutonniere. "Ta-da!" Seriously. He said "Ta-da!"

"Are you taking her to the prom?" Uncle D asked. "Or are you two getting married?"

Brad's smile was wistful, showing fang. "Can we do both?"

I wasn't so chipper. Yesterday, we'd taken advantage of school being out for Labor Day to power shop. But with only ten days till the premiere party, Uncle D's ruling was "no go." We'd have to try again. Maybe look into express-ordering something online.

"I do look kind of like a lounge lizard. But that's no reason to waste the suit." Brad extended his hand to me. "Would you do me the honor of this dance?"

"There's no music," I said, feeling awkward.

"There's always music," he replied, "if you listen carefully enough."

Brad had been trying out lines like that, now and then. Trying to get into character. So far, he sounded like a typical fan boy, not like the headliner.

"Don't you think dancing is kind of silly?" I asked.

"Don't you think it's kind of silly to dress up in a tuxedo and not dance?"

It was hard to argue. I climbed off the chair, Brad spun me, and then we were waltzing, a skill I owed to the valiant six-week effort of a middle school gym teacher. Brad was good, a strong lead. I gazed up into his red eyes. He seemed ready to confide something, and I took a side step, not ready to hear. It would be simpler to keep dancing.

As Uncle Davidson cleared his throat, we broke apart.

Truth was, I'd forgotten for a moment he was standing there.

"Quincie, honey," Uncle D said, "mind if I have a word with you?"

It was an ominously parental question.

Excusing himself, Brad ducked out of the room to change clothes.

My uncle waited until he was gone and motioned for me to follow him to the foyer. For privacy, I supposed.

"The clock's ticking," my uncle began, using his index finger to wipe dust from the photo of Mama and Daddy. "Brad's been busy with the food, and. . . . Don't get me wrong. You've done a top-notch job of managing him, but I'm ready to settle for a good cook and let Ruby play to the crowd."

Ruby *again*. Yuck. It was so unfair! Besides, what if she and my uncle broke up? Talk about your personal-professional wreckage. Uncle D wasn't thinking straight. He was in some kind of sex haze. It was my duty as his niece and my mother's daughter to save the restaurant. "But when Vaggio was alive, you loved the vampire chef idea."

Uncle D's face fell. "Honey, Vaggio was a born showman. Brad's not. We can still call him 'the vampire chef.' He'll just stay offstage. But we need a star."

"Ruby, you mean." I took refuge behind the hostess stand. Going off about her to my uncle wouldn't help my cause. "One more chance," I begged. "I can do this."

Uncle D considered a moment before backing down. "Okay, okay. You're such a doll, always there for everyone else. Me especially. You can try again with Brad's makeover. One more try."

I beamed at him. "Thanks!"

With that, he retreated to the kitchen. A moment later, I heard his laugh, mingled with Brad's. I opened Frank at the hostess stand to make a new to-do list.

The phone rang, catching me off-guard. "Sanguini's: A Very Rare Restaurant," I announced. "May I help you?"

"This is Detective Sanchez. Who's this?"

Oh my God, I thought, the police. Sanchez, Sanchez . . . I didn't remember a Detective Sanchez, but the days surrounding Vaggio's murder had been such a blur. Maybe he was the guy who'd come with Detective Bartok to the memorial service.

"This is Quincie Morris," I said into the phone.

"Quincie, good. Listen, this call is confidential." It was an order, not a question. "I don't want to read about it in tomorrow's paper or see it on News 8."

I tightened my grip on the receiver. "Understood."

I heard the detective take a drink. Coffee, I figured, imagining him, mug in hand, hunched over his messy desk at the station. Come on, I thought. Whatever it is, tell me.

"I'm calling to urge you to be careful. The victim . . ."

"Vaggio," I said, glancing at his birthday picture. "His name was—"

"Mr. Bianchi was an older man, but he was in good health. At the time of the crime, he may have had his guard down. The perp—"

"Perp?"

"The murderer, the shifter. It's probably someone he knew. Which means—"

"It's probably someone I know, too."

FAITH

"Quincie!"

I jerked my head up as Mr. Wu slammed his Econ book on my desk.

"This is a class, not a slumber party. Next week, try caffeine like the rest of us."

Mr. Wu was the one teacher who hadn't adopted The Tone since Vaggio's death. At first I'd been grateful. Now, not so much.

The bell rang, and I peeled out of there, turned into the filling hallway, and ran smack into Vice Principal Harding.

"Good morning, Miss Morris."

Damn. "Good morning, Mr. Harding."

"It's not too late for you to consider home-schooling."

Having just been awakened by the Econ teacher in front of my whole first period, I had to admit the idea sounded more appealing than it had initially. But then I remembered the main reason I liked school. He was in my next class.

"I'll keep that in mind," I replied, dodging Harding on my way to my locker for my English book.

When I slid behind the desk next to Kieren, he was leaning over his notebook, the highlighted short story spread open in front of him. That's when I remembered. Friday's scheduled quiz. Hawthorne. "Young Goodman Brown." I used to calendar out all of my assignments in Frank, but lately, I hadn't bothered. I didn't even have Frank with me today for some reason. I put my hand on Kieren's forearm. "I didn't do the reading—"

"Again?"

"I had to work. What's the story about?"

"It's this sledgehammer study in symbolism with—"

The bell rang and Kieren paused, glancing at Mrs. Levy.

"Go on," I whispered.

But before he could, Mrs. Levy said, "Please put your books and notes under your desks." She passed out the quizzes to the first person in each row, and they passed them back. After a few more instructions, everyone got to work.

I squinted, trying to make some sense of the questions. The words looked blurry. What was it with English teachers and their desperate need to quiz? I wondered. Did they enjoy torturing students? And where did Kieren get off judging me, just because I wasn't spending every minute with my muzzle buried in a book? The whole thing was so stupid, so pointless. So juvenile. I, I didn't . . .

"Do you need to go to the nurse?" Mrs. Levy whispered at my shoulder.

"Why?"

"You're crying," she told me in The Tone.

MYSTERY

When I finally escaped the nurse's office—guest-starring the school counselor as "I thought I'd say 'Hi' and see if you wanted to talk"—Kieren was leaning against the manila hallway outside the door, his backpack slung over one shoulder.

"Shouldn't you be in calc?" I asked.

He took my English book. "I thought we'd cut out for the rest of the day. Do you need to stop by your locker for anything?"

I glanced at the text in his hand. What was this, the 1950s? He didn't usually carry my books. Of course he didn't usually cut school either. I had been planning to hit chem before taking off, but so what? "I guess not."

"Good." Kieren turned toward the front door. "Let's go."

Passing the fountain next to the administration office, we fell silent and walked together out of the school. Not one secretary had looked up.

"You feeling better?" he asked halfway down the walk.

"Better?" I spread my arms, soaking in the freedom, the sunshine.

"Than you were in class this morning?"

Oh. "It was nothing. Cedar, I guess. My eyes started watering."

"You don't have allergies. I do, and I'm fine today." Stepping onto the parking lot, he added, "If you don't want to talk about it, I understand."

It was my second offer to talk in the past hour. Inside Kieren's truck, I tuned the radio to a Los Lonely Boys song and listened to that instead. I had no idea where we were going, but I was so glad to be with him and not in chem that it didn't matter.

The mystery held while we stopped by his house. Miz Morales waved to me and handed him a picnic basket at the front door. Brazos bounded out behind Kieren and leaped into the truck to sit between us. Then I rolled down the passenger-side window, changed places with the overgrown pup, and scratched behind his ears as he panted out the window. I'd always wanted a dog, but Uncle D had said we worked too much. Brazos loved me though, and it was mutual. "Your mama doesn't mind that we're cutting?"

"No, not at all. She sends her love."

When Kieren turned into the white-stone pillars at the entrance, I understood.

It was September 6, my parents' wedding anniversary, the day I'd set aside to honor them. The day they'd become a family. Kieren had remembered when I'd forgotten. He must've assumed I'd been emotional in English because of today's date.

Last year I'd counted down the days, starred the box on my September monthly calendar page in Frank.

This year, *nada*.

What kind of an excuse for a daughter was I?

The cemetery was small, lined with a wrought-iron fence, located about twenty minutes from my house. The older tombstones stood upright, many faded, several guarded by stone angels or lambs. The first year, Kieren and I had taken a bus, and last spring, he'd driven us. The picnic basket and Brazos's company were new.

My parents' graves were shaded by a magnolia tree, marked with a single flat stone. It had a built-in vase, and before I could feel worse about not bringing flowers, Kieren reached into the basket for a plastic-wrapped bouquet of pink sweetheart roses and a bottle of water. I knelt down to scratch Brazos's belly while Kieren busied himself. He set up the flower arrangement, spread a moss green blanket, put out a snack of sliced apples, pecans, feta, and whole-wheat crackers on moss-green paper plates, and handed me a moss-green paper cup with matching napkin. Our names had been written in curly silver metallic ink on our cups, both with hearts over the respective *I*'s. We sat side by side, and Kieren poured me some sparkling cider before noticing the panting dog.

"Sorry, boy." He opened the basket again for another bowl and a bottle of water.

"I take it your mama packed the basket for you."

"What makes you say that?" he asked.

I laughed.

Instead of talking about Wolves or vampires or Sanguini's or the murder investigation, Kieren and

I remembered my parents. Remembered how Mama could eat a heaping plate of Vaggio's calamari all by herself. Remembered how Daddy would spend hours combing the beach in Galveston for seashells. Remembered how long they'd debated over what colors to paint the house before settling on green and purple. Remembered how often they'd held hands. It was the best I'd felt all day, but then I realized, who would come here with me when Kieren left for the pack? From the way Miz Morales had been talking, it sounded like he'd be gone long before next year.

During an electrical storm later that night, watching the news with Uncle D, I learned that there was a flash flood warning for Westlake Hills and that a dead body had been found near the Four Seasons Hotel on the hike-and-bike trail.

It wasn't far from here to that new murder scene. Within walking distance.

Walking distance from my house. Walking distance from Kieren's.

I thought back to Detective Sanchez's warning and hit MUTE on the TV remote. "It was Mama and Daddy's anniversary today. Kieren went with me to the cemetery."

"You could've asked me," my uncle said. "Or Brad."

"Brad?" He'd never even known them.

Uncle D glanced at the coverage of college foot-ball. "He's 'Bradley Sanguini.' That makes him family now. Like you said about Vaggio."

Remembering the fuss he'd made when I'd hung Vaggio's photo, I was surprised to hear my uncle say that. "You and Brad really seem to have hit it off," I said.

"And you've had a tough day," Uncle D observed, "visiting your parents' graves and all. Can I get you something? A glass of wine?"

I thought about the body just found, about loved ones lost. About Kieren. I wished I could mute my emotions the way I had the TV. It would be easier not to think at all, at least not for the rest of the night. The wine could help. "Sounds good," I replied.

POOF!

I understood that Brad had to get the food order in, but did he have to look at his watches every minute? The restaurant supply shop on South Lamar wasn't that far away after all. Flipping through the rack of classic uniforms, I asked, "Do you have to *do* that?"

"Do what?" he asked, all innocence.

I didn't bother to bicker about it. "I wish you could just turn into a bat. Like *poof*! Very dramatic. That would solve all of our problems."

"Would it?" Brad looked amused. "I'm sorry to inform you that only the Old Bloods can do that. Changing into a wolf is easy, a beginner's trick. Any well-established vampire—say, between fifty and a hundred years old—can dissolve into mist or dust, too. But a bat is harder. The extra mass has to go somewhere. It's a bigger, more powerful magic."

He sounded like he knew what he was talking about.

I paused, giving him my full attention. "Is that true?"

Brad's fang-filled smile had become familiar. "I did my homework, remember?"

He had mentioned that.

"Oh! Oh, wait," I said, back on task. "Check this out." Holding my breath, I pulled out a men's large tall uniform. Black with red piping. Cotton, not polyester.

He shook his head. "Too 'Iron Chef.'"

I exhaled.

"Try not to take it too hard," Brad told me. "My faith in us is eternal." He reached out and tucked a stray hair behind my ear. "How's that broken heart doing? That boy going out of state to school?"

"I don't have a broken heart. It's . . . he's still my friend."

"Quincie, we all have first loves," my chef replied. "At the time, they seem more significant because we haven't had anything to compare them with yet. But there's a reason they're called 'first.' More often than not, there's a better love yet to come."

"It sounds like you've been there," I observed. "What happened?"

He took my hand in his, and we headed toward the door. "She's dead."

I didn't know what to say. "Does it hurt?" I asked. "I mean, like it did at first?"

"If anyone threatened someone I loved with that kind of pain," Brad replied, "I swear I'd kill them myself."

"I'm sorry," I said. "That's lame, I know—"

"It's not lame," Brad replied. "It means a lot. Any other costuming ideas?"

It seemed considerate to let him change the subject, and I gave the question some thought. It was Saturday afternoon, and most shops would be closing in another hour or so. Plus, the U.T. game would be over soon, spilling burnt orange onto the streets.

Was Kieren there with Meghan and his dad? They always ordered season tickets, and his mama usually worked on Saturdays. Kieren hadn't mentioned football in ages.

These days, attending a college game was probably too normal for him.

He'd never wanted to be normal, I realized. Go to U.T. and study whatever, then get a regular job and marry a girl like me who did something as common as restaurant management. He talked about his inner Wolf, how dangerous it could be. Needing a pack so he wouldn't hurt anyone, especially me. So he wouldn't have to worry all the time. I believed that was part of it.

But big picture, Kieren had always wanted a different life, a special life. He'd earned it with his were-studies. He'd been born to it on his mama's side. He'd become the Wolf pack scholar, mated to some bitch he hadn't even met yet.

Would Kieren miss me the way Brad missed his first love?

Did Kieren even think of me that way? I'd been so sure, on and off, but now . . .

Brad's hand in mine felt cool, reassuring. Like we walked this way all the time.

On the way out, I brightened. "There's this one place, Second Chances, on Burnet. They might have a black trench coat—"

"Trench coats," Brad said, escorting me to The Banana, "are for gumshoes, perverts, and rainy days."

Playing Dead

Uncle D had taken off tonight with Ruby, saying he'd be home before 1 A.M. His good deed for the day: letting Travis off early. Mine: helping Brad clean the kitchen, which had gone faster than we'd expected. We didn't usually work on Sundays, but with the re-opening next weekend, there was so much to do.

Yawning, I shuffled upstairs in the dark, holding fast to the handrail. I loved the house, what had been my parents' house. It wasn't big, two stories, built in the 1930s, very art deco, expanded in the '60s and again when I was five. The furnishings were a combination of pieces passed down from both sides of the family, including souvenirs from my parents' many jaunts to Central and South America. Mostly of the basket, rug, and figurine variety. Mama had been particular about wanting things just so, and that's pretty much how we'd left them. Except for her indoor trees and the hanging ferns that had died off over the years, the place hadn't much changed.

Turning into my darkened bedroom, though, something stank to high heaven. My first thought was sewage leak; my second, decomposing animal. I'd never seen a mouse, or anything but tiny milky lizards. But maybe a squirrel had burrowed into the attic. Still, that didn't explain the wafting garlic scent mixed in with the ick.

One step. Another. Reaching for the light switch, I tripped over a *body* and, flailing, landed with an *oomph* on a huge hard-shell animal, which hopped three feet into the air, knocking me off, back onto the still body. Screaming, I scrambled against the door, which slammed behind me. It, it . . .

The animal was a shifter. It had to be. It was too damn big not to be. But werepeople were of the furred persuasion, occasionally feathered or scaled. Not hard.

As for whoever on the floor, I had no idea.

Steeling myself, I hit the lights, illuminating the dead-looking body of Clyde—a spray bottle in one hand, something pink in the other—and a five-and-a-half foot werearmadillo. No blood, but pungent fluids of a yellow-and-brown nature on the floor, close to the 'dillo. Even more disgusting, some of the sticky residue was on me.

Kieren had once told me that shifter transformations varied in pain, mess, ease, and smell from wereperson to wereperson and species to species. This guy's odor was like months-old sweaty gym socks. And the 'dillo himself? He looked like a cross between a huge gecko and a huge hog. Cowering with his head pulled into his shell, tail curling to meet it. Poor thing looked scared to death. Of *me*.

It was hard to tell, but I thought the 'dillo was Travis.

A squat beige candle was burning on my night stand. Garlic scented.

"Quincie, it's you!" Clyde sat up to look at me. "We just heard you come in, and we kind of panicked—"

"Kind of." I stayed where I was, back to the door, fighting to calm myself.

"He shifted," Clyde continued. "I cut the lights, and—"

"Played dead?" I raised my chin. Kieren often said dominance was the foundation of most exchanges between mammals. The higher up the food chain, the more complicated the game. In my own bedroom, having been scared out of my wits, I was not feeling inclined to defer.

"We thought you were him!" Clyde went on.

It took me a minute to process that. "My uncle?"

"The vampire!"

I should've guessed. "And what are you again?"

Clyde shut his eyes like he was about to go catatonic, so I took on the kind of voice a vet might use while administering annual shots. "Easy." The words felt idiotic, but . . . "Some of my best friends are were-people." My best friend. "You can tell me."

"'Poss, 'possum," Clyde replied, rising. "I'm a were-opossum. I can play dead in human or 'possum form. That's . . ." He pointed. "Travis. He's a werearmadillo."

I'd figured that much out. "Kieren sent you."

Travis uncurled and bobbed his bulky head.

"We're supposed to vampire-proof your house," Clyde explained. "We started here, in your bedroom, and thought we'd work our way out. We would've asked first, but nobody was home and Kieren said it was an emergency, so—"

"How did you get in?"

Clyde shrugged. "The front door was unlocked, which isn't very safe. Vampires have to be invited in, but there are all kinds of other—"

"Yeah, I know." What was with Uncle D? I wondered, not for the first time. Didn't he have the good sense to be afraid?

Sidestepping the stinky, sticky fluids, I paced the floor of my bedroom. My nice, normal, sensible bedroom, the one I hadn't bothered to redecorate since I was about twelve. A full-sized canopy bed with a calico-print bedspread, matching nightstand and dresser in an eggshell ivory, moth-chewed Oriental rug that clashed with the bedspread, a rattan chair. And Travis . . . God, I'd never seen a wereperson in animal form before.

Something occurred to me. "Vampire-proof it how?"

Holding up the spray bottle, Clyde answered, "Holy water for the window panes, and in the bag, we've got—"

"What's in your other hand?" I asked.

"Uh."

"Are those my *panties*?"

"Well," Clyde replied, "we might have gotten a little distracted."

Oh my God. "And where the hell is Kieren?"

"Investigating something at school that will just blow—"

"You," I said to Clyde. "Put. My underwear. Down."

"And you," I told Travis, grimacing at the yuck on my hands, "fix yourself."

Glancing down, I noticed the shredded boy-clothes, recognized them as remnants of what he'd worn to work. "No, wait," I said. "I'm going to grab some of my uncle's things and bring them back here. Then I'm going downstairs so you can do whatever you need to do to become a fully clothed, boy-shaped sophomore again." I pointed at the bag on the floor, the one with a Celtic cross half falling out of it. "Take that with you."

After Travis and Clyde collected their antivamp kit and left, I blew out the garlic-scented candle, cracked my windows, cleaned the floor, showered, scrubbed the tub, and then decided I'd feel better with some protection handy.

But the gun I'd inherited from Grampa Crimi? Gone. I'd always kept it in my chest at the foot of my bed, beneath the Mexican blankets. I double-checked between the folds to be sure.

Kieren had warned me against carrying it, bringing it to work. Because the gun couldn't protect me, he'd said. Because it could be taken away.

Playing Dumb

*K*ieren's truck pulled up alongside me as I was walking to school the next morning. I'd gone the long way, through the residential neighborhood, to think.

"Hey," he called from the driver's seat, "get in."

I kept walking. I hadn't called or e-mailed him last night, hadn't counted on seeing him until I got to school, hadn't figured out yet what I wanted to say.

"You're mad?"

I didn't slow down.

"Yeah, Clyde called me when he got home. I'm sorry, Quince." He stopped and leaned over to open the passenger side door. "I'm trying to apologize."

I didn't get in. "They were in my bedroom!"

"They weren't supposed to do that, just go into your house like that."

"Clyde was rummaging through my underwear!"

Kieren's expression became dangerous, possessive. It was clear Clyde hadn't bothered to mention that tidbit.

I pressed. "I want my grandfather's gun back."

He narrowed his eyes. "The gun?"

"Don't play dumb," I replied, lowering my voice as a jogger sped past. "You knew where I kept it, you sent in your little friends, and now it's gone."

"Quince, please get in the truck."

"No."

He killed the ignition, got out, and joined me on the sidewalk. "Did you see them take it?"

"No. But they had a bag with them. It was probably in the bag."

Kieren put his hands on my shoulders. "I did not take the gun. I swear to you I didn't. I didn't ask Clyde or Travis to take it either, but believe me, I'm going to talk to them this morning about a few things."

I shrugged him off, tired of touching that only went so far.

"We're going to be late for school," Kieren said.

"I'm not going."

"But—"

I turned around, started walking. "I'm going to work instead."

"What about the gun?" Kieren called.

As if he didn't know.

When I stormed into Sanguini's kitchen, Brad was seated at the island reading *A Taste of Transylvania* from The Eclectic Ethnics Series. "Something wrong?" he asked.

I stopped in the middle of the room, realized I was standing exactly where I'd . . . where Kieren had first discovered Vaggio's body, and jumped back. "Men suck."

Brad seemed to consider this. "Not all men, just the really good ones."

I folded my arms, unappreciative.

"Do you want to talk about it?" Brad asked, so solid, secure, *there*.

I took the stool next to his. "Why does everything have to change?"

"Not everything does," he replied. "Some things are forever."

I mulled over how Kieren was going to leave me, how I wasn't sure I could trust him anymore. "Not in my life."

"Maybe," the chef said, "it's your life that's the problem."

I thought again about Kieren, how long I'd pined for him.

Maybe Brad was right.

Bat Man

I had to give Brad directions to Barton Creek Square Mall, just south of downtown, off MoPac, the gateway to the western suburbs. It was our latest expedition in search of a vampire chef ensemble. Neither of us spoke from the back door of Sanguini's until we reached the *primo* parking space near the movie theater.

"I'm sorry," I said. "I know you probably think I'm neurotic, but let's just go."

"Something wrong?" Brad asked from the driver's seat, his hand on the key.

Inside waited a Nordstrom, a JCPenney, a Sears, two Dillard's. An Abercrombie & Fitch, Eddie Bauer, and untold shoppers.

It was possible that we might be able to find something Brad could wear at one of the various retail outlets. But it would be mass-produced, easily copied, and potentially familiar to any Tom, Dick, and Hernando who strolled through the door.

Like minestrone, not special enough.

"Too risky," I said. "We can't have some random customer show up looking like your twin." I upped the air-conditioning. "You know, I hate to say this, but I'm starting to think a vampire restaurant in Austin makes no sense. Why would a vampire want to live here anyway?"

"Your uncle was brainstorming that with me the other day," Brad replied, turning the radio on to an old Lyle Lovett song. "For media interviews. You know, PR for the restaurant. The way we figure it, because sunshine weakens vampires, most masters have avoided the Southwest. That means it's a power vacuum, a growth opportunity. Plus, humans have been moving to this region in big numbers, and hunters tend to follow the herds. Not to mention the live music, a thriving downtown, bats."

I fought a smile. "You said only really old vampires could turn into bats."

"But that's the thing about vampires," he said. "Eventually they will get old enough, and the natural bats would make swell camouflage. Besides, vampires are a fringe population, and Austin is a tolerant place. Think about those people here who're campaigning for undead rights. That wouldn't happen in most Texas cities. In College Station or Amarillo, locals would come after any known vampires with blowtorches." Brad shifted the SUV into reverse. "Where to now?"

"Um." With only three days left, I was running out of options. Fast.

A moment later, turning onto the frontage road, Brad suggested, "Why don't we stop by my place? I'd love to show you what Ian and Jerome have done with the remodel. We could share a bottle of wine, celebrate the breakthrough in the case."

"The case?"

"The murder investigation," he clarified. "Didn't you hear? APD announced today that they were close to making an arrest."

It was news to me. I'd had drinks late last night with Brad, skipped school this morning, and hadn't talked to Kieren since yesterday when we'd fought about

Grampa Crimi's gun. Kieren. . . . I hadn't checked my cell for messages every five minutes, hadn't checked my e-mail every fifteen. But God, how I'd wanted to.

"Quincie, aren't you pleased?" Brad asked, looping around to Highway One North. "That nightmare will be over soon."

"It's a lot to take in," I replied, trying to sound calm. Were the police planning to arrest Kieren? I wondered. No matter what, I'd loved him so long.

"How about my invitation then?" Brad countered. "It's a beautiful old house. Not as beautiful as you, but I think you'll like it."

Clearly, Brad was hoping we'd do more than check out the carpentry. It dawned on me again that he was technically a grown-up and I wasn't quite one, though our age difference was no more than that between, say, a freshman and a senior.

Still, Uncle D seemed to approve. And I'd never bonded with anyone so fast, maybe because. . . . Lately, life had been so uncertain, and Brad shared my love for Sanguini's. With Vaggio gone and Kieren going—which maybe was for the best—Brad was inviting me in. I said, "I'll take a rain check."

PREY OR PREDATOR

*F*or the last couple of days before the debut party, I blew off school to help with last-minute whatever. But Brad had pushed me aside as taste tester in favor of Uncle D, and they got psycho secretive about the new menu, hushing whenever I peeked into the kitchen. It was so annoying.

"Oh, come on," I'd begged. "Tell me. Let me try something." Uncle D was the boss, but didn't both of them need my opinion? It was like they thought I was only there to run errands, answer phones. "Just a little bite."

They'd laughed like it was the funniest thing I'd ever said. Uncle D had poured me a placating glass of Cabernet, and Brad had offered to serve me a sampling from the final menu tonight, September 12. The suspense was killing me.

I ran into Uncle D and Ruby coming out of the front door.

"How's it going?" I asked, my shopping bag in hand.

Uncle D shook his head. "It's too late to do the two or three days of run-throughs with the staff. They'll pick up menus and ingredient lists at 9 A.M. tomorrow and try to memorize them by sunset."

Ruby trailed her long nails down my arm. "How's your vampire chef coming along?"

Witch. I jiggled the bag and tried to look optimistic. "Under control, but it's not like we *need* someone to play vampire, do we?"

"I'd hate to cut the midnight toast," Uncle D said. "It's the crowning moment."

I just couldn't win. "Well, have fun." I pecked his cheek, taking a giant step back when Ruby leaned toward me. Then, waving bye-bye, they left.

At my fave booth, I admitted to myself that, whether I liked it or not, Ruby *was* Uncle D's only choice to play the head vampire.

Brad strolled in from the kitchen, fangs glistening, eyes glowing red, receding hair still pale blond—he'd refused to consider dying it. He was sporting his standard business casual. Geek chic, like he'd just stumbled out of a tech office on a casual Friday. Brad was tall, too, I realized. I'd noticed before of course, but tonight he wasn't slouching. Shoulders straight, he had to top 6 feet 4 inches.

"Hi!" I handed him the bag. "This is going to look stupid on you, but try it anyway. I'm desperate."

He humored me. The traditional chef's hat—white, pleats—made him look too stretchy overall and he'd never clear the hallway ceiling.

I buried my face in my hands, defeated. My uncle had his heart set on Countess Ruby Sanguini.

Brad slipped the hat back into the bag. "How about I give it a shot?" He rapped his knuckles on the top of my head. "Quincie?"

I set my chin on my palms. "Hm?"

"Your uncle is paying a lot of attention to Ruby, but we're a team, right?"

We had been spending a lot of time together.

"You've already laid the groundwork," he said. "Let me do my part."

What was left to lose? Ruby would show up tomorrow looking her usual vampish self anyway, and I was out of ideas. "Okay," I said. "Thanks."

At least someone in my life was cooperative.

"It's settled then. Hungry?"

"Thirsty, but I can eat." And I was curious.

Brad excused himself and returned carrying two menus. *Two.*

I tried to imagine. Tomorrow morning, the tables would be rearranged. Tomorrow afternoon, staff would arrive to rehearse and the dance floor would be installed. Tomorrow night, Sanguini's guests would be seated and served . . . something.

"Prey or predator?" Brad asked at the table.

"Beg your pardon?"

His smile had a confidence I hadn't seen since that first night with the police. "Have you yet been blessed into a vampiric being?"

"No," I said, amused. "Not yet."

He handed me the prey menu. "It's about the dance. Predator and prey. That's what seduction is, dancing."

Was that sexy? I'd give it a C-/D+, like the ones I was getting in all my classes back when I bothered to regularly attend. Borderline sexy. "Can I see both?"

He handed me the predator menu, brushing his long fingers against mine. "I've prepared a tasting for you, a sampling of everything we'll serve."

Setting the menus side by side on the table, I ran my fingertips over the white, pressed leather, traced the gothic-style crimson lettering, and toyed a moment with each of the gold tassels. Opened both menus.

~ Sanguini's ~

A VERY RARE RESTAURANT

PREY MENU
(select one in each category below)

antipasto

portobello mushroom pâté

roasted eggplant oregano

primo

corn conchiglie salad
in virgin olive oil over butterhead lettuce

mozzarella, gorgonzola, and parmesan ravioli
in wild mushroom sauce

secondo

eggplant parmesan

roasted tomato and wild mushroom stew
in red wine sauce and vegetable stock

contorno

roasted asparagus

tomato and heart of palm salad

dolce

tiramisù

crème brûlée

~*~ Sanguini's ~*~

A VERY RARE RESTAURANT

PREDATOR MENU
(select one in each category below)

antipasto

foie gras terrine
marinated in Cabernet Sauvignon,
sautéed with brandy in balsamic vinegar

veal tartare

primo

breaded pig's feet à la Sanguini's
in Merlot and onion cream sauce with fettuccine Alfredo

sautéed porcini and veal kidneys
in veal stock reduction with orecchiette

secondo

blood and tongue sausages with new potatocs

boar's head pie with boiled eggs in a graham cracker crust

contorno

ham and peas mozzarella

sweetbreads with spinach

dolce

rice pudding blood cakes

chilled baby squirrels
simmered in orange brandy, bathed in honey cream sauce

Everybody's Got a Dark Side

Oh my God! To think Brad had talked for hours about banal issues like northern versus southern versus pan-Italian and nixing heavy cream sauces because of the climate.

He touched the tip of his tongue to each of his fangs, then started showing off.

It wasn't like being served dinner so much as being offered tribute. Each petite selection—two or three bites only—perched on a bone-white china plate.

Time and wine to clean the palate between.

We didn't talk, Brad and I, alone in the dining room. He made offering after offering, and I accepted. He strolled between my table and the kitchen, my wine glass—Chianti with the prey dishes, Cab with the predator—never less than half full.

"These will make up the whole wine list," Brad mentioned in passing. "Nothing else will be offered—no coffee, no tea. We'll serve water only upon request."

The prey menu first, few surprises, a sampling of the best dishes I'd vetted already. The predator menu, more daring, designed to titillate. Amazing for someone who wasn't even Italian. Even Vaggio would've been wowed.

I refused to be intimidated, though. The veal tartare was exquisitely raw, the foie gras terrine predictable, the main courses—from pig's feet to boar's head pie—a toe-to-top invitation for the eager carnivore, the sides obligatory, but the desserts. . . . The desserts were something else and something *else,* at least one of them was. I lingered over the last bite of rice pudding blood cakes. "You're brilliant!" I declared. "Bravo!"

"Ready for the grand finale?" he asked.

I met Brad's eyes, realizing how used to the red

contacts I'd become. To me, that's what he looked like. Otherworldly, but rooted in khakis and oxfords. Saucy, but safe. "Bring it on."

Big talk. When the culinary virtuoso returned with the chilled baby squirrel, simmered in orange brandy, bathed in honey cream sauce, I . . .

"Problem?" Brad asked.

It wouldn't taste bad. Everything had been delicious, decadent, and on the predator menu, devilish. The other dishes had been tiny, but on this one, he'd gone all out. Problem was, it still looked like a squirrel. A darling squirrel, skinned and naked, curled like it was trying to keep warm. It was enough to turn a cattle rancher vegan.

"I'm pretty full."

That had sounded neutral enough, I hoped. Not like someone with bile pooling at the base of her throat.

"It's not about volume, not this particular dish. It's about the drama. A certain type of predator will order the squirrels to show that despite the hokey restaurant—"

"Hey!" Though he had a point.

"And clichéd counterculture staff, it's just possible—"

"He's a vampire," I finished, impressed. "I get it."

"Or she's a vampire," Brad put in.

I gave him a wry look.

"What?"

"Nothing. Ruby, I guess. She's such a freak."

The fingertip tracing a blue vein in my wrist was light, cool, attentive. It made me wonder how it might feel somewhere else.

"But we're in the freak business," he replied. "Aren't you dressing up?"

Uncle D had mentioned that vamp duds and accessories would be available tomorrow in the break room in case anyone needed to augment their wardrobe. He'd looked at me in my typical blah denim and cotton T as he'd said it, though he wasn't pushing. "I have to, I guess. It's a huge deal, the party, and we have so many new hires. My uncle's going to need my help."

Brad was still touching me. "You've had to grow up fast."

This was a date, I realized, Brad and me, sitting together in the black leather booth in my otherwise empty restaurant. This time, I didn't feel guilty.

On impulse, I threaded my fingers between Brad's, squeezed, and let go. Unscathed. I wasn't Vaggio's buddy anymore, I realized. Wasn't Uncle D's side-kick. Wasn't Kieren's girl. The honor-roll nobody, little orphan Quincie.

I felt adult. In control. Tantalized.

That in mind, I picked up my fork, picked up my knife, swallowed my revulsion, and ate the squirrel.

Delicious.

secondo

Forever Young

The afternoon before the debut party, Clyde found me in the break room. I had been quizzing three of the waiters, Xio, Jamal, and Mercedes, on the new menus and explaining to Xio that Brad hadn't seemed inclined to add a whole-wheat pasta dish.

"I've got a delivery for you," the Opossum said, jiggling a bag. "From Kieren."

It was impossible to look at Clyde and not remember him clutching my pink panties. But I took the bag, peeked inside, and smiled in spite of myself.

It was a plastic container filled with habanera-stuffed olives, like Vaggio used to make. I guessed Kieren had turned to his mama's favorite caterer. I slipped into the chaotic kitchen, stashed the olives in the fridge. Brad wasn't in there at the moment, which was unusual, but he was around somewhere.

After much internal debate, I decided it was only polite to call. Taking a glass of Cabernet with me, I went back into the break room, where the servers were doing the happy dance over their mental brilliance. Then I went into Uncle D's office instead.

"Hi."

"Hi," Kieren answered, his phone voice cautious.

When did this become so hard? "I wanted to say thanks for the olives."

"You're welcome."

I took a sip. "What's wrong?"

"Nothing," Kieren replied. "I just got back from the police station. More questions. The same questions over and over."

The police hadn't called me back in. I remembered what Brad had said about a pending arrest. "Detective Sanchez?"

"Who?" He paused. "No, it was Bartok and Matthews, the ones who came to Vaggio's memorial service. You know, who questioned us the night he died."

"What do they want?" I asked.

"I don't know. Matthews said something about running my DNA—"

"Can they do that?"

"My lawyer says he'll try to fight it, but that's our worst-case scenario."

When did Kieren get a lawyer? I wondered, putting down my glass.

"They don't want me hanging around the restaurant," he added, "what with the cops and everything."

Who were "they"? His parents?

"But I'm going to try to sneak out later tonight, okay?"

His parents. Jesus. What should I say? "Okay. Um, is there anything else you want to tell me?" I wasn't about to use the word "confess."

"Like what?" Kieren asked.

I closed my eyes. "Nothing."

He hung up, and so did I.

It was then that I remembered the hang-up phone call on the night of Vaggio's death. I guessed I'd been so traumatized it had slipped my mind before now. I realized that anyone familiar with the restaurant redesign would know the phones were in the foyer, the break room, and the office. They'd know that at least for the moment of the call I hadn't been in the kitchen. If it was Vaggio's murderer, maybe he'd seen an opening, taken a chance on entering through the back door while I was elsewhere in the building.

It might be nothing, I realized, but I should probably tell the police.

I decided to talk to Uncle D first, though, when we had a moment. After all, if Kieren needed a lawyer, maybe I did, too. The list of people who'd seen the inside of Sanguini's up to that point was a short one. Outside of my family, just Kieren, the renovation folks, and some delivery people. I lifted my glass and drank deeply.

Speaking of deliveries, as if life didn't suck enough, a beefy guy—the name sewn onto his shirt read "Sid"—appeared at the office door looking for a manager to accept responsibility for a fortune in wine. "He's not here." Uncle D had left a few minutes ago to pick up more napkins. "But Davidson Morris is my uncle. I can sign."

"There's nothing here about leaving all this with some underage . . . niece."

He'd said it as though my familial claim was suspicious, eyeing my drink.

"Whatever you say," I replied. "Go ask for Sebastian at the bar."

"I don't know," Sid said. Like he was going to leave and take the wine with him.

I stood, slamming my glass onto the desk, breaking it at the stem. "Damn!" The top rolled off, exploding as it hit stained concrete. "Damn it!"

"Quincie?" Brad asked, hurrying through the door to my side. "Are you hurt?"

"I . . . no, I'm. . . . *He* won't leave the wine."

Brad introduced himself to Sid as the head chef and signed on the clipboard.

"Babes in Toyland," Sid muttered, wandering out.

Ignoring him, Brad led me around the less perilous side of the desk. "I'll ask a server to clean up in here."

"I, I'm stupid and clumsy."

"Compared to you, Garbo herself was an ox. With the party hours away, it's only natural for you to be nervous. *I* am, and it's not my mom's legacy on the line."

It was a relief having someone who understood.

"And that boy?" the chef asked. "Is he still upsetting you?"

"I guess."

Brad adopted a movie vampire accent. "Don't vorry. You can *count* on me."

BRAD THE IMPALER

I feel like an idiot," I said. Maybe it was because I was wearing fishnet stockings, black leather hot pants, and a black leather bustier. Maybe it was the makeup—black lip and eyeliner, alabaster base and powder that covered my freckles. As for the four-inch heels? God, I could barely walk.

I didn't have a moral objection to dressing provocatively. It just wasn't my style. But for Sanguini's sake, I could try it. I was open-minded. Sort of. And as a little kid, I'd always loved Halloween. Tonight, I'd refused any jewelry, though, skipped nail polish, and rejected dye, pulling my hair into a face-lift bun. "I'm sure I look like an idiot, too."

Ruby, even more appallingly appareled and drenched in musk, pushed to sit, slim legs crossed, on the office desk. She's the one who'd needled me into trying on the bustier in the first place. "You look better than you ever have before."

I wished I could check myself out in a mirror, but the restaurant didn't have any, not even in the restrooms. If something got stuck in someone's teeth, it was supposed to be considered thematic. Maybe it was good, though, that I couldn't see myself. I might go full-barrel chicken if I did.

"It's the four-inch heels," I said. Don't get me wrong. We were selling sex, at least metaphorically, along with the ambiance, food, and liquor. I was even grudgingly grateful to Ruby for her help. But I couldn't function up so high, and the soles were so slick that I'd be sure to wipe out by close. I kicked off the shoes and tugged on my new red cowboy boots instead.

Yanking up my bustier, I sighed. "Let's focus on the restaurant."

"Your precious family restaurant, your uncle's precious family restaurant," Ruby chanted. "You'd think it was Tara. 'As God is my witness, I'll never' blah, blah, blah."

I wasn't certain if she and my uncle had had a spat or if she was looking long-term to cash in on the place as community property. Now that I thought about it, though, the misconception that Uncle Davidson owned Sanguini's could go a long way to explaining how he'd managed to land her in the first place. I mean, paunchy, thirtyish guy, going nowhere, with barely twenty-something, budding dominatrix, likewise going nowhere. So, I clarified. "My grandma and grandpa Crimi's restaurant, my mother's, mine. My uncle is just managing it for me until I hit twenty-one."

Not that I wasn't planning on Uncle D staying as long as he wanted. Not that he'd ever bail on a family obligation. Not that it was any of her business anyway. But I was weary of Ruby trying to make me doubt myself. She was such a drain.

Uncle D popped his head into the office, still sporting his aloha shirt with Levis and Birkenstocks. "Chop, chop, ladies. It's almost sunset. Quincie, honey, double-check the waitress station."

"The one behind the hostess stand or the one behind the bar?"

"Both!" he replied as I ducked out. "Ruby, double-check the kitchen for hairnets."

"Ball caps okay?" I heard her ask.

Was she on the payroll now?

A couple of the servers, Simone and Mercedes, both leggy goddess brunettes, looked up when I passed the break room. They were folding crimson napkins into bats. Their mascara-laden eyes blinked at my appearance—not drastically distinct from theirs, but before tonight my idea of a fashion risk had been wearing a jewel-tone instead of a black or white T-shirt.

"Quincie!" Simone exclaimed. "You look—"

"Wicked!" Mercedes finished.

I laughed, blushing. "Gotta run."

It'd meant a lot to me and Uncle D, how many of the old timers had returned, quitting the jobs they'd taken while we were shut down for renovations, saving him tons of little-to-spare angst and training time. Acts of faith. The handful of newbies on the wait staff had each been assigned a vet to follow, and they'd rotate that way for the next couple of weeks. Everything would be fine, I told myself. It had to be.

Sergio, the expeditor, caught me to avoid a full-on collision. "Easy," he said. "Remember, no matter how much you're in the weeds—"

"Never show it," I finished. "Walk the same pace. Remain calm."

Sergio's job was to hurry the food on the line and run it to the tables. Another veteran returned to the fold. "You're holding up like a champ," he told me.

"Holding up?"

"It's hard on all of us, getting through tonight without Vaggio, but the show must go on, right?"

"Uh, right." I needed another drink.

"Your mama would've been so proud of you, lamb chop."

I kissed his cheek. "Thanks."

At the end of the hall, I parted the crimson velvet curtains, revealing the dining room. The mood lighting had been turned on. Subtle, shadowy. Jazz played through hidden speakers. Tables and booths had been preset as had a small dance floor.

Tick, tock, I thought. Almost time.

That's when I heard the chef's voice. "You look good enough to eat."

In the center of the dance floor waited Bradley Sanguini, vampire. His suit was a dark gray, accentuating his height and slender build. I could see only one dress watch gleaming beneath the cuff, but I'd bet the twin above it was just as fancy. No makeup or other affectations, at least not beyond his trademark fangs and red contacts. Maybe a touch of base. Wait, yep, and eyeliner and lip liner, both smudged to blend. It worked for him. As did the hint of blue blush to accentuate the cheek bones, make the face seem more defined. Even his widow's peak juxtaposed against the twenty-something face hinted at a vampire's classic immortality while evoking history, experience. He looked confident, at ease, standing in the middle of the dance floor as if he owned it, every inch the latter-day un-dead Fred Astaire.

"Nice suit," I said.

His smile showed tooth, and we had a Count Sanguini after all. One so striking, so awe-inspiring I couldn't think of what my uncle had sent me in to check.

"Sunset," Bradley whispered, slipping on a skullcap. "I can feel it." He breathed the words like he could almost see the ash violet, candy cotton clouds against a pale blue and apricot sky. But the truth was, with its windows bricked, Sanguini's seemed to exist totally separate from the natural world. He couldn't see jack.

"A little more Jedi than Lugosi," I replied. "But color me enthralled."

Bradley smiled. "I should change to cook," he said, strolling past.

He smelled like olive oil and paradise.

"Incoming victims," Yanira called from the hostess stand.

This was it. I grabbed a fresh glass of the house Cab from Sebastian. *Carpe noctem!* I thought. Seize the night!

CARPE NOCTEM

Sanguini's sparked, then sparkled, moving as if in a waltz. Guests, many dressed for the occasion, were greeted by Yani and escorted to their two- or four-tops, where a server asked each if they considered themselves "predator" or "prey" and then presented them appropriate menus. One guy walked in with a spiderweb tattoo covering his entire face, a woman with porcupine quills threaded through her nostrils. A tall, very tall, and solid-looking red-haired man, neatly trimmed beard, dressed to the nines circa 1912, introduced himself in a pronounced Irish accent, "Mr. Stoker, party of one." We had no fewer than four Mr. Stokers that night, one of which was a leather-jacket-sporting miniature Pomeranian, carried in a matching purse, whose owner acted heartbroken that we weren't "Pomfriendly." And they weren't the most extreme or the most innovative. I'd never seen so much leather and feathers and fishnet and lace.

As Uncle D and Ruby worked the room, I tried to blend, which wasn't so difficult. Shadows abounded, and partygoers became absorbed in the experience. They grimaced and giggled and gloried at the descriptions of predator dishes, yet both hunters and hunted devoured every bite. The dance floor—center stage for seduction.

Not that I could just watch. I restocked wait stations, supplied an extra corkscrew, refolded napkins, wasted a minute on a custom order for some skinny woman bitching about carbs, removed a dining chair to make room for a guest in a wheelchair, politely explained there was no freaking way any of the servers would be merrily crooning "Happy Birthday to You" in either Italian or English, and chatted with one of Vaggio's exes, Celeste, who was at table five with her daughter. I was fetching a stray spoon from the floor when Sergio tapped my shoulder.

"Sorry, lamb chop," he said, holding a tray topped by a bowl of tomato and wild mushroom stew and a plate of pig's feet. "But I've gotta keep running food, and there's a woman with a problem in the hall. Something about the restrooms."

I tossed the spoon in a catchall at the wait station. "On it."

In the dim hallway, I saw her before she saw me. Plump, grandmotherly, sporting fang marks on her neck—a temporary tattoo. A lady who'd never let on to her bridge set how much she enjoyed erotic horror novels, but then again, wasn't worried about running into any of them tonight.

What now? I wondered. No toilet paper? I'd checked the supply half an hour earlier. The condom machines? This might be a place for role-playing lovers, but you had to give reality its due. I *prayed* she hadn't slipped, thrown up, or had some kind of bowel eruption. The last thing we needed was food poisoning rumors, a trumped-up lawsuit, or heaven forbid, a cockroach. "May I help you, ma'am?"

"Oh!" She straightened, clasping hands. "Yes, dear, it's about the peeing."

"The peeing?"

In reply, the lady gestured to the two restroom doors, which earlier today had been marked "M" and "W," but now "Predator" and "Prey." The "Prey" door had a cross on it. The "Predator" door didn't. Unisexy. Nobody had warned me.

"I don't mean to be a prude. The food is fantastic, and I, well . . ." She lowered her voice. "I have certain fantasies, you know."

Falling under the category of too much information.

Waving her hands, she continued, "But I just can't go with men—"

"I'll guard the door." As emergencies went, I'd seen worse.

An hour later, I dropped off a tray of dirty dishes, and the kitchen was chaos.

"Where's Travis?" Uncle D yelled in the crowd. "Clyde, where's Travis?"

"Didn't show," Clyde replied, water spraying dishes. "But no sweat. I'm cool."

My uncle threw his hands into the air and stormed out of the room, muttering.

"Quincie," Bradley called from the stove. "A homeless guy stopped by the back door a while ago, asking for a handout. Said his name was Mitch and to tell you howdy."

"Did you feed him?"

Bradley nodded, stirring. "He looked hungry and harmless. I'd given him some leftovers a few weeks back, too. Was that bad?"

"No," I said, relieved. "Not bad at all."

Big picture, things were going as planned, though Uncle D—in head-to-toe black mesh and massive amounts of hair gel (I nearly died laughing)—did have to step in when the intoxicated date of a city council member made a grab for a waiter's ass, thus causing said waiter to dump a plate of sautéed porcini and veal kidneys on the mayor's lap. And at the hostess stand Yanira did suggest Uncle D install a sign in the foyer to read:

Cell phones
will be eaten

THE PRINCE OF TRANSYLVANIA

I refilled water and wine glasses, helped the busers clear tables, and conferred in the hall with the lead singer from Luminous Placenta about placing a ruby-and-diamond engagement ring on her girlfriend Amber's blood cakes.

A number of guests, in tones both hushed and boisterous, were discussing the two bodies found at the hike-and-bike trail, one last night and another the previous Friday. I overheard a few rumors. One gruesome, one hysterical, one that made me cringe.

I tried not to listen whenever someone mentioned Vaggio.

Once I realized the servers were clearing dinner plates, I ducked into Uncle D's office to check the digital clock. Two minutes until midnight. Bradley was to make his grand entry during the dessert service. It wasn't like he needed me for the midnight toast, but I wanted to be there. As I turned to leave, a shadow flexed on the wall. "Kieren?"

"I was looking for—"

"I've been in the dining room or kitchen all night. It's been crazy, but, hey, thanks for coming." I'd never considered myself a babbler, but I was so euphoric the words just tumbled out of my mouth. "Did you sneak out? Oh, we've got to get back. Wait until—"

"Quince, stop, *stop*. I'm here to—"

"Later," I said, slightly tipsy.

"Now." In the shadows, Kieren's eyes reflected like mirrors. "Listen, I think it's Ruby. I think she's the vampire. I think she killed Vaggio, or at least, she was in on it. Quince, I think she's using the restaurant as a beacon to her kind, a hunting ground. I'm not quite sure what. Maybe Vaggio saw something. Maybe . . ."

Giddy mood fading, I couldn't believe he'd used the phrase "beacon to her kind."

Kieren, not being a mind reader, kept talking.

"She's been seeing your uncle since about the time the whole vampire remodel came up. She's never at your house. She's hardly ever let me within a hundred feet of her, up or downwind. Coincidence?"

I thought back to what Uncle D had said about Ruby wanting to turn vampire for real but then remembered. The night of Vaggio's murder, she'd been swimming au naturel with Uncle D at Hippie Hollow. "Ruby has an alibi. She—"

Kieren growled at me, and I shrank back. He'd never growled at me before.

One moment he was haunting the shadows, I realized, the next he was in my face.

Detective Sanchez had said the killer had been someone, a shifter that Vaggio had probably known. Kieren had known Vaggio. Kieren was half Wolf. Kieren had discovered Vaggio's body. Kieren had been covered in blood. Kieren also had been acting weird, really weird, and I wasn't an idiot. I knew the wereworld wasn't all puppy-dog eyes and man's best friend. I couldn't stay in denial forever. Even the police suspected him.

I inched backward till my hand hit the brass doorknob.

"Maybe I was wrong about Ruby," he admitted,

"but my instincts are screaming. Something about you seems wrong, smells wrong."

And now I was insulted, too.

"Quince, you're . . . When's the last time you showed at school? Did you know that five students are missing? Eight or nine people in the neighborhood?"

I'd heard the waitstaff talking, but they'd always hushed when I walked into a room. I hadn't realized how high the number had climbed. "The cops—"

"Don't understand what they're up against."

"They know Vaggio's murderer is out there."

"Out there," he repeated. "Do you realize he could be in here, in this very building at this very moment."

That did it. "I have to leave."

I took off down the long hall, past the doors marked "predator" and "prey," walking fast, running when I heard him closing in behind me.

We burst, me first, Kieren on my boot heels, through the velvet curtains leading to the dining room. Everyone stared—guests, wait and bar and hostess staff, Ruby and Uncle D—then returned their attention to the main event.

Everyone except Bradley, who was dressed as he had been before the party began, only more flushed, more vibrant. He stood once again in the center of the dance floor, a glass of red wine perched in his right hand. Making a speech about the foolishness of those who'd entered freely and of their own will.

Bradley waited until finishing his thought to turn and address Kieren. "You," he roared. "You are not welcome among the blessed."

Kieren laid rough palms and finger pads on my forearms, and I goose-pimpled beside the air-conditioning duct. "You know me, Quince." He let go before I could shrug him off. "Nobody knows me like you."

All eyes watched him exit with a dignity humanity lost long ago. Unbeatable, that's what his body language said. There was just somewhere else he'd rather be.

As the door closed behind Kieren, the vampire chef raised his glass in a toast, leading all those gathered in doing the same. "I dedicate this drink to the countess of this fine establishment, she whose destiny is this dream."

Bradley Sanguini raised his glass to me.

Sink Your Teeth into Sanguini's

by Sandra Divine
RESTAURANT CRITIC

AUSTIN, TX   Sanguini's: A Very Rare Restaurant proved itself not only rare but rarin' at a lucky Friday, September 13, debut party. This reviewer, called upon by hostess and server to self-identify as "prey," was consumed by the horror and romance of South Austin's hot new cutting-edge vampire restaurant. The so-safe Italian staples found on my own menu, however delectable, paled in comparison to those on my companion's, a self-defined "predator." As She Who Split the Squirrels, I must say my status shifted that night, and having embraced the tutelage of master chef Bradley Sanguini, I'm forever eager to answer his dark call. *Five stars.*

"I Could Have Danced All Night"

*T*onight, Saturday night, would be our first of regular business. Not a handpicked guest list, just whoever had called to reserve a table, including probably a reviewer or two who was miffed at not having been invited to the debut. Tonight, the tables would turn over. Higher volume. Higher stress. Higher stakes.

This afternoon, I was indulging in a glass of Chianti with Uncle D in his office when Clyde appeared at the door with news of Travis's death and to give notice.

"Travis *died*?" I turned the idea over in my mind and felt nothing. Shock, I supposed. Like with Mama and Daddy. Vaggio. But no, this felt somehow more numb. Empty. Maybe because I'd only liked Travis, rather than loved him. "What happened?"

Clyde glared at me like I should already know.

"You're quitting?" my uncle exclaimed as if that was the only part he'd heard. "But it's opening night."

I glanced at the clock. Two P.M. At that very moment, Clyde was supposed to be starting in on the dishes from the pastry and prep.

"If you quit now," my uncle added, "do you think you're going to walk out of here with a good recommendation?"

Clyde's nose twitched.

"I can wash dishes," I told my uncle.

"You shouldn't have to do that, honey."

Uncle D made out one check for Clyde and another for him to give to Travis's family. As Clyde reached to take the money, though, my uncle jerked back his hand. "Stay for dinner tonight and there's another hundred in it for you."

Clyde smiled down at us, revealing sharp, tiny teeth. "I don't think so."

"One fifty," my uncle countered.

"No."

"Three."

My eyes widened.

"Just tonight," Clyde said.

"Deal."

"I won't close," he added. "I'm leaving with the last guests."

About a half-hour before opening, Sebastian took a break from bar inventory to drop by the office and relay that Bradley had a surprise for me in the private dining room.

It was small compared to the main one, but with matching décor—the faux painted "castle" rock walls, candlelike wall sconces, crystal chandelier—and big enough to hold a six-top, which, with leaves, could seat twelve. Overwhelmed, Uncle D had held off on booking it until Halloween.

When I walked in, Bradley offered me a single red calla lily. "For you."

I loved lilies. They reminded me of champagne flutes, weddings, and funerals.

"I'm sorry that boy tainted last night."

"It wasn't horrible," I said, mostly trying to convince myself.

"Yes," Bradley argued, "it was. You deserve so much more, someone who'll offer a real, long-term commitment. Someone you can trust. Promise me that if he comes back you'll be more careful. You'll ask for help."

When did Kieren become someone I sought protection from? When had Bradley become that protection? My life was changing so much, so fast. My life, and for that matter, my restaurant.

I briefly closed my eyes. "I promise."

Then Bradley showed me a handwritten sheet. "Now then, I'm going to run this by your uncle, but I'd appreciate your thoughts first."

Flattered, I took a moment to adjust my neckline. That night, I wore a midnight blue lace gown—it matched the carpeting—of my own choosing over a light beige thong. The lace had seemed like a bang-up idea when I went out shopping that morning, but now my nipples were starting to chafe.

I wasn't the only one who'd upped the wardrobe a notch, though. Bradley planned to augment tonight's toasting ensemble with a full-length black cape.

Catching myself staring, I lowered my gaze to read. It was a proposed bio for the menu insert. Somehow, that project had slipped my mind. Already a wash for the debut party . . . I swear, my brain was a colander these days.

Thank God for Bradley!

Bradley Sanguini

HEAD CHEF

Sanguini's: A Very Rare Restaurant

Bradley Sanguini was born a human in the United States, to a heartland family that perceived him as something less, something twisted, when in truth he was destined to be more.

Of his own will, Bradley offered himself to the blessings of the vampiric life.

All vampires drink from human vessels. Some vampires bless a select few by wetting the tongues of the chosen with their own blood. Yet it was not enough for Bradley to walk free of humanity's constraints, morality, rules, and limitations. Not enough if he walked alone. And so, he made a most unexpected decision.

Bradley sought to feed his prey, not just to feed on them. He embarked on culinary studies in Paris and then found a home at Sanguini's in Austin, Texas.

It is here, night after night, that Bradley hunts and feeds. It is here, night after night, that Bradley welcomes his fellows to dance and play. It is here, night after night, that Bradley beckons foolish humans to taste true darkness. Here that he seeks all those worthy of blessing and one to be his bride.

"Do you think that's sufficiently diabolical?" he asked. "Only one bride when Dracula himself took three?"

Did he mean me? I wondered, or was he just flirting again? I pretended to give the matter serious consideration. "One seems like enough for anybody."

LITTLE FREDDIE MUNSTER

On her way back from seating a couple with waist-long dreadlocks and wearing head-to-heel silver spandex, Yanira tapped my elbow. "Some people are asking to say hi to you at the hostess stand," she said.

"What people?"

But she didn't hear me. The crowd created a steady hum, punctuated now and then by uproarious laughter. A large man wrapped in chains had stepped between us on his way to the restroom. Then I found myself trapped between two servers in front of a couple of tables pushed together to accommodate a large party. They'd all dressed as historical figures commonly rumored in the supermarket tabloids to be vampires. I was able to ID a King Tut, a Janis Joplin, a Ulysses S. Grant, and a Mary, Queen of Scots.

Trying to circle around, I found myself blocked again, this time by a quartet of midfortyish six-foot-tall women—at least I thought they were women—standing arm in arm chatting about our chandeliers. All had been body-painted—as in hair, skin, lots of skin, no clothes whatsoever—in a sparkly twilight violet. Matching nail polish, spiky heels, and . . . yes! Matching sparkly twilight violet bikini panties. Whew. Otherwise naked except for the paint and belly rings all featuring the same charm: a skull and crossbones. Bully for them. In this town, it was legal for women to go topless so long as they didn't cause a riot. Besides, Uncle D had ditched the **NO SHIRT, NO SHOES, NO SCAMPI** sign with the remodel.

Reaching the hostess stand, I saw them. The reason Yani had summoned me.

Looking at little Nathaniel, you'd think "cherubic." Huge blue eyes, red curls. His wardrobe: Baby Gap meets Buster Brown. His folks, Bobby Dale and Jeannie Fredericks, both taught Sunday School at my church.

He was an assistant vice president at the downtown bank where my family had our accounts. She made a mean potato salad. "So," I cooed, "what brings y'all in?"

"Dinner," Jeannie said, looking at me like I'd done something questionable. "We wanted to show our support. No matter what people may say—"

"Congratulations," Bobby Dale blustered. "The place looks interesting. It's Nate's birthday, so we said he could stay up late today, though he may—"

"I'm five!" Nathaniel shouted, holding up a handful of fingers.

The entire restaurant got the message.

"Five!" he continued. "Five! Five! Five! FIVE!"

Experience informed me that this chant could go on through dessert. Not that I was ever a babysitter type, but most kids are fine. Give 'em crayons and a chocolate sugar bomb of a dessert, and call it done. I adored Kieren's little sister, Meghan.

"Five!"

But Sanguini's wasn't a family-fare establishment.

"Five!"

Word of mouth mattered, and it was opening night for regular business.

"Five!"

Jeannie exclaimed, "That's my big boy!"

"Five!"

Bobby Dale asked, "Can you believe he's five already?"

"Five!"

Yani returned from seating the body-painted.

"Five!"

Where was Uncle D?

"Five!"

And just when I couldn't take it a second longer, my hero swept onto the scene in his midnight toast ensemble. "Why, I believe someone is five today."

Slack-jawed, Nathaniel gazed at the vampire chef.

Bradley didn't squat like a lot of people do when talking to little kids. "Life," he declared instead, "merits celebration. Do walk this way."

Escorting the Frederickses through the dining room, not bothering to make eye contact with any of the guests, he'd already established himself as their savior. No one would mind the break in suspense before midnight.

Bradley led the family into the private party room. It was unoccupied and soundproofed.

"I love you," I whispered, only half kidding, as he shut the door on them.

"Tell Yani that I recommend Mercedes take the table. She has infinite patience and, better yet, a brown belt."

"In a Glass Darkly"

*K*ieren was seated alone at table nineteen, a two-top along the south wall, his back to the front door. Chianti and eggplant parmesan untouched. A manila folder in front of him on the satiny black tablecloth. A small turquoise-and-silver crucifix dangled between his collarbones from a thin silver chain.

I circled the dining room. Uncle D and Ruby were busy chatting up Mercedes's dads. Sergio had his hands full running food. Sebastian was in the weeds at the bar. I'd thought off and on all day about Kieren. Now here he was again.

Pausing at the hostess stand, I whispered to Yani. "Could you do me a favor? Holler for the bouncers from the back lot."

"This is about your ex, isn't it? I'm sorry I seated him. But there he was and—"

"He's not exactly my . . . I mean, it's okay. I don't even know if—"

"Ian and Jerome will toss him—"

"Let me see what he says first," I said. "We don't want a scene."

I made my way into the dining room, slipped into the chair across from Kieren's.

He slid the manila folder to me.

What could it hurt to play along? I opened it, flipping through the documents he'd brought, nodding for Simone to fetch me another drink, making a mental note to remind her to card the customers. "If this is about Ruby—"

"It's not."

Frowning, I returned my attention to the paperwork. It was a collection of printouts from websites. He had enclosed a bibliography. A few entries caught my eye, those that had been highlighted in yellow:

Johnson, Henry. "Beyond Sashimi and Tartare: Culinary Expressions of Neovampirism." *The Gothic Gourmet* (December 1986): 3–12.

Johnson, Henry. "Hearts at Stake: Gender Politics Arising in Post-Vampyric Infection." *Demonic Digest* (July 1967): 2–31.

Johnson, Henry. "Vampirism and Attention Deficit Disorder: Ramifications Related to Social Interaction, Cross-Species Relationships, and Iron Deficiency." *Preternatural Psychology* (March/April 1994): 2–19.

In that vein, the list went on and on.

"He wrote these," Kieren explained. "Henry Johnson, Bradley Sanguini, whatever you want to call him—Sanguini's chef. Some of the Web pages hosting these documents haven't been updated since the 1990s. Some of the articles were first composed when flappers were considered trendsetting."

I tapped an impatient blue-glitter fingernail on the tablecloth. "Oh, come on. Last night you thought Ruby was a killer vampire. Tonight, Bradley." Bradley hadn't even been living in Austin when Vaggio was murdered. "Who will it be tomorrow? Me? Will I be a homicidal vampire, too?"

"Wednesday night," Kieren countered, "a man carrying an ID for a Vaggio T. Bianchi bought a case of silver bullets from a guns-and-ammo shop owned by some local Wolves who got in touch with my mother. The Gamma working backup tailed the guy downtown —"

"Not funny," I said, trying to act natural. But it was coincidental that this revelation was linked to one of the few hush-hush Wolfish things I happened to know about. "Uncle D packed up Vaggio's stuff and shipped it to his family in Chicago."

"You think I'm lying?"

I rubbed my eyes, not caring if I smeared the makeup. "I don't know."

Simone cruised by, setting a fresh glass of house wine on the table. "'In a glass darkly,'" she said. "Compliments of the chef."

A nearby four-top turned over, and an aging, B-list movie star was seated with his scarcely postpubescent eye candy of the week. It was time to wrap this up. "Kieren—"

"Quince, look at yourself."

"Can't," I said, palms up. "No mirrors."

The small joke had been a miscalculation. He picked up his fork, a possible weapon, and I raised my glass, flagging for backup.

"Where's your planner book?" Kieren asked. "Where's Frank?"

"I, I think it's in my uncle's office. On the desk." Truth was, I wasn't sure. How could that be? Frank and I were codependent. But I hadn't checked my calendar lately, my tasking pages. My fingertips itched for the leather cover.

"You've changed," Kieren went on. "I'm not only talking about wardrobe, though"—he studied the taut lace semicovering my breasts—"I must say . . ."

Damn him, I thought. "Why are you even here? You said you were leaving."

"So what?" Kieren replied. "You're trying to beat me to it? Shut me out of your life so it doesn't hurt so much when I go?"

"*I've* been here the whole time," I protested.

"No, you haven't! I don't know who *you* are." He took a steadying breath. "Quince, this guy you're messing around with is dangerous."

"I'm not 'messing around' with—"

"He's evil. And you're, you're slipping away. Listen to me, please. I'm begging you. I'll get down on my hands and knees if that's what it takes."

It was such a puppy thing to say.

"Stand and come with us." It was more a series of grunts than words, and I wasn't sure which of the bouncers had spoken. Ian and Jerome seemed to function as a unit. Sporting standard black business suits, they'd self-exempted from dressing like the rest of the staff. But what with their bald, sunburned heads, jaundiced skin, and noses that rivaled Cyrano's, they nevertheless looked sufficiently Sanguini's "Sir?"

Kieren didn't acknowledge them. "Somebody poisoned Brazos's food," he told me. "I found him this afternoon, dead in his doghouse."

Brazos? I waited for the hurt to come, but it didn't. Like it hadn't when I'd heard about Travis. But, why not? I'd loved that dog like he was my own.

Kieren set down his fork and looked at me like I was the one who'd died. "I'm not giving up on you," he said as he rose from the chair, then left.

Seconds later, Uncle D materialized at my side. "Honey, are you—"

"He didn't hurt me."

"But he was aggressive?"

I nodded, took a deep breath, and told him about the forgotten call from the night Vaggio had died.

"I hope you understand," my uncle said. "Tomorrow I'm going to have to give APD a heads-up on this, let them know what's going on."

I nodded again.

TIPSY

At 2 A.M., as Yani locked the front doors, I skipped through the dining room. Our official opening night had been a smashing success! Every reservation had showed. Customers had raved. Bradley had sailed through the midnight toast, flirting with his red eyes. The kitchen's pacing had been perfection, Kieren's brief challenge had been squashed, and Clyde had stormed out early, like anyone gave a damn.

Cleanup was a snap. Every last server and barkeep offered kisses and hugs on their way out, girls and boys both, all beautiful and ballsy and sky-high on tips. Before I knew it, the kitchen staff had taken off, too. Exhausted and cussing a blue streak, the sign of a magnificent night. I told Uncle D and Ruby I'd catch a ride home with Bradley and went to look for him in the kitchen.

I found him stooping to clean the range. It wasn't a chef duty, but he was meticulous. He tossed the rag aside as I danced in, floated, singing "We did it!"

Tipsy and loving it, I beamed at Bradley, the heavens, the hells, rejoicing in that which was Sanguini's. I spun in the room, which was spinning itself, and laughing, sagged against the counter. "We did it," I repeated. "Bradley?" I turned to fall into his arms and teetered.

THE MORNING AFTER

I woke up beneath Bradley's cape on the frayed floral sofa in the break room at about 7 A.M., feeling every inch like I'd just eaten a full-grown goat with the fur still on. Fully sober for what seemed like the first time in weeks, which was wretched.

I had a vague memory of Ian and Jerome tossing out Kieren and another, even more distant one, of Bradley ditching me in the midst of a drunken stupor.

Both possibilities made my squishy gray brain feel like it was being pummeled by multitudinous ball-peen hammers.

Where was everybody?

I struggled to my feet and left the break room for the prey restroom, where I was glad Uncle D hadn't installed a mirror. I let the cold water run to icy and began splashing until I could think clearly and was sure the majority of my makeup had been washed off. Blinking away the wet, I gasped as my gaze traveled down my body.

Last night, I could've sworn the dark blue lace had been evocative, demure, but that morning, not so much. The material had torn at the front hem of my skirt and strained to breaking over my right hip. It had ridden up, too. Scandalously.

Grabbing my dress at the hem, I yanked it over my shoulders and tossed it in the trash. Leaving on my beige thong and boots, I, mostly naked, retreated to my uncle's office where I retrieved a spare T-shirt, shorts, and Nikes from a bag I kept in the top drawer of the filing cabinet. Dressing quickly, I fell into my desk chair.

In the great annals of hangovers, it wasn't much comfort that this would go down as number one.

The open ledger caught my eye. The entry for the

check made out to Travis's family. Travis had died. Sweet, clumsy, shy Travis. Dead. He'd been only sixteen years old. I felt stunned, shaky. But I'd already known, hadn't I?

God! When was the funeral? Had Uncle D ordered flowers or had he asked me to do it? Or should we have brought food to the house? After Mama and Daddy died, people brought food. Casseroles, tamales, a brisket, two hams, pasta salads. Microwave three minutes. Microwave five. A shrimp platter, cold cuts, cheeses, cheesecakes, pies.

Rubbing my temples, I went into the restaurant kitchen. If Vaggio were here, he'd make sausage lasagna. I'd seen him do it thousands of times. I opened a cabinet and took out a pan, grabbed a bottle of olive oil. Went to the refrigerator and stared inside.

It was no use. The stock wasn't Vaggio's. It was Bradley's. I slammed the refrigerator door shut.

Poor Travis. His family. It's awful, death. Not just the dying, the intrusive rituals surrounding it. Here I was, worrying about flowers, food. I should've known better. At death, flowers were ugly, food went to waste, and words seemed insignificant. But, I guessed, the worst thing to do was nothing. The worst thing would be if nobody cared.

I wanted my mama. I wanted my daddy.

I wanted Kieren.

Poor Kieren. He must've been miserable. And I, *I* couldn't even remember having told him last night how sorry I was. Not about Travis. Not about, oh, Brazos either. Did I still believe Kieren could be Vaggio's murderer? I wondered, blinking back tears. The last couple of nights I'd been almost sure. This morning, I had no idea what to think. I couldn't . . . this was . . . it was . . . I hardly knew myself anymore.

In the break room, I tried to call Kieren. No answer. Uncle D at home. No answer there either. At Ruby's, the line just rang and rang.

Bradley! I had to talk to Bradley. He'd help me sort through it. These past few weeks, he'd made time for me. Listened. He wasn't obsessed with a Wolf pack or Ruby the skank. He'd been around long enough to have an informed opinion but not so long that he couldn't be objective. I'd written his contact info in Frank. God! Where *was* Frank anyway?

I searched everywhere, under a pile of Xio's menu notes on the coffee table, beneath the couch. Back in Uncle D's office, on top of the filing cabinet, under the desk, in the trash can—finally finding it beneath the overflowing IN box. I clutched Frank to my chest, rocked back and forth, kissed the leather cover, and then opened it to the contact pages so I could copy Bradley's address onto my palm.

Then I remembered what Kieren had said last night, that Bradley was the bad guy. Kieren had found some stuff on the Internet. But how many Johnsons were there anyway? Besides, it wasn't like you could believe everything you read online. And Bradley hadn't even been in Austin on the night of Vaggio's murder.

Had he?

To be safe, I called directory information for Paris, Texas, and got the number for Chat Lunatique, Bradley's previous employer. Pretending to be a magazine editor, I said I needed to double-check the spelling of the name of the chef on duty August 9. For a rave review, I'd explained. A hostess working brunch transferred me to a manager who confirmed that on the night of Vaggio's death, H-E-N-R-Y J-O-H-N-S-O-N was some three hundred miles away cooking up *coq au vin.*

On the way out, through the kitchen, I reached into the refrigerator again, this time for the habanera olives from Kieren. Comfort food. I popped one in my mouth, managed to down it, then, coughing, fought nausea as it tried to force its way back up.

Bad olives, I thought. Disappointed, I tossed the rest.

It was then that it occurred to me why the pastry team hadn't arrived at 5 A.M. to start on tonight's pasta and whatnot, why the prep team wouldn't be arriving within the hour to chop and slice.

It was Sunday.

Sanguini's was closed on Sundays.

"Hallelujah."

My Own Free Vill

I took a bus to Bradley's neighborhood. North side of the river, close to downtown, la-di-da old money back in the day, already regentrified. Many of the houses could be called mansions, where fountains flowed and where, now that I thought about it, a twenty-something chef out of Kansas City, Missouri, by way of Paris, Texas, newly hired by Sanguini's, shouldn't have been able to afford more than a carriage house rental.

Walking past one estate after another, I licked my lips. God, I was dehydrated.

Rounding a landscaped corner, I looked up at Bradley's house, its beige stucco façade, forest green wrought iron balcony rails. It stood two-and-a-half stories high on a hill. Three flights of cracked concrete stairs rose from the sidewalk to the front door, cutting a hard line through the lawn, the portico flocked on either side by statues of sleeping dragons. Pushing my damp hair off my forehead, I trudged up and rang the bell.

Jerome answered, dressed in green and peach paint-splattered overalls, taking in my presence with what I could've sworn was resigned sorrow. He grunted, shutting the door in my face. He and Ian had been re-modeling Bradley's house, I remembered, which did nothing to explain his behavior.

"Um, hello?" I paced, taking in the welcome mat, the square copper mailbox. After a while, I got bored and sat on the top step. Sleepy, achy, I should've called first.

Finally, Bradley opened the beveled glass front door, backed by a green velvet curtain that looked reminiscent of the crimson ones at the restaurant. He smiled at me, and I wondered if he'd taken those few minutes to put in his contacts and fake teeth.

"Enter freely and of your own vill," he intoned.

"Haven't we already played this game?" I forced myself into a standing position, shuffled inside. I'd come to talk, but now that I was in my vampire's lair, the words were slow coming.

As lairs went, it wasn't bad. Crystal chandelier in the foyer, columns rising to arches framing a stairway to the second floor. A left turn took me into a parlor designed around a hand-carved fireplace mantel, and I noted the matted and box-framed antique bowie knife hanging above it in the spot o' honor.

The clocks caught my attention. Three grandfathers in the entry. Ornate. German. Three more—smaller, black with gold trim—had been poised in a row on the mantel. Each set to mark different hours. None ticking. Which, considering my head, was good.

Bradley offered his arm. "Milady."

I took it. "Nice digs."

"Headache, baby?" He led me to a leather club chair and drew the curtains closed. "Does that help?"

It did. The sunlight had been too intense for my exploding brain cells. I glanced around. The dining room, which I could see through French doors, was empty, unfurnished, and it looked like the chandelier—another one, but brass with teardrop crystals—needed to be rewired, some stray beige paint removed. The sunroom, which was visible through yet another set of French doors, housed a tropical-looking day bed and had been curtained off. A boom box on the hardwoods, just a few feet away, played something jazzy.

"You collect?" I asked, examining the crystal clock paperweight on the cocktail table beside me.

"Time intrigues me. Our most squandered resource."

"I don't squander."

"I know. It's one of the first qualities I appreciated in you."

Maybe it was my headache, but I had nothing to say to that. I just waited for the moment to pass, impatient. Bradley let it linger.

"Hair of the dog that bit you?" he asked.

Did I look that bad off? I hadn't even had breakfast yet. "Water."

He brought Cabernet instead, a glass for each of us, and pulled up the leather club chair's mate to sit across from me, his trouser-clad knees bumping my bare ones. I shivered in the air-conditioning. One whiff of the wine, though, cleared my head.

He raised his glass. "To us."

"Us."

"I'm sorry about abandoning you like that last night. I didn't want to take advantage. I needed for you to come to me."

We each sipped, and then he took my glass and set it with his on a cocktail table.

"You're trembling," Bradley said, resting his long fingers on my thighs.

Later, when I woke up, I remembered kissing. I had a vague recollection of sucking on Bradley's wine-coated tongue while he sucked on mine and of feeling colder. And I thought we'd drunk some more. But I may have been dreaming.

The wine had been drugged, though. That seemed likely, given that the next clear realization I had was that someone had tied me to the rusty antique iron frame of a twin bed, no linens, in an unfinished basement with no windows, lit by a single dangling bare bulb. The room was otherwise barren except for a furnace.

I was alone.

My gym clothes were gone, and in their place, I was wearing a long, gauzy white nightgown. Sleeveless. Classy in a Victoria's Secret kind of way. Beige thong in place. Barefoot. Virginal, bridal, sacrificial. In a rush, I knew . . .

God help me, I was going to die.

Sheep's Clothing

*F*ear ached in my joints and burrowed into my belly. It wormed its way inside my neck muscles and held them tight. Oh, God, I thought. Oh, God, oh, God, oh, God.

Minutes later, someone opened the door at the top of the stairs.

Ruby looked down at me like I was yesterday's fish. "She's awake."

"She has nearly risen," Bradley said, turning the knife in his hand so the blade flashed from the bare bulb. "She is nearly blessed."

Worse, a wolf—Wolf?—large for an animal, brushed past Bradley and loped down the unfinished stairs to bare his choppers. The dusky blond fur bristled. Dear Lord, I prayed, please don't let that wolf be Kieren.

Bradley walked as if he were ambling down to check the pilot light. He clucked his tongue, and the wolf heeled.

"Um, uh," I whispered. "Wh-what—"

Bradley crossed the room in a blink. Taking the flat side of the knife, he caressed my throat. "So fresh. Baby, how about a drink?"

"No, thanks." I shuddered. "What do you want?"

Bradley withdrew the blade. "What does anyone want? Power, devotion, dear friends, dead enemies, real estate, a place in the world, a purpose, a community . . . " His hazel eyes flashed red, a trick beyond contacts' technology. "Someone to love. Someone to love me."

Before I could stammer a reply, Bradley lunged toward the headboard. I scrambled to the far edge of the bed, my back to the wall, but then he began using his knife to saw into the ropes. My breath came fast, but I couldn't afford to hyperventilate.

"There, there," Bradley said. "Even if I couldn't stop you, and I could, don't try anything rash. Even if you got past me. . . ." He nodded in the direction of his guard dog. "And him, Ian and Jerome are at the top of the stairs."

Once the rope securing my right hand had been sliced down to a string, I pulled free and yanked the left as well. The thicker ropes, untouched by Bradley's blade, strained against the bed frame, bending it before breaking. "What the hell?"

"That's the second time you've asked me that. The first was the night we met, remember?" Bradley laughed, moving to sit beside me on the bed. "And once again, I'm thinking: What an appropriate question." He looked contrite. "You'll have to forgive me this. I told my men to secure you so you wouldn't wake up alone, panic, and do yourself some harm by trying to break out. I didn't mean to cause alarm."

He still had the knife, though. Bradley must've realized that was a matter of concern because he snapped his fingers and Jerome glided down the stairs without acknowledging me to take it away.

"Soon," Bradley went on, running the backs of his pointed nails across my cheek, "once you've proven your mettle, we'll move you upstairs in style."

"Mettle?" Such an old-fashioned word.

Bradley clucked his tongue again. In response, the wolf rose up on its hind paws and changed. Smooth, fluid, graceful even. Its legs lengthening, its paws re-forming into hands, its spine becoming that of a man, and its face that of pushing-thirty, paunchy, familiar Uncle Davidson.

My uncle Davidson. Dressed. Hawaiian shirt and cutoffs. Birkenstocks. No mess, no fuss, no fluids. No cracking bones or strangled cries. No stench. Just, done. Fangs extended. Eyes red.

Werewolves could shift between Wolf and human form. It was natural, Kieren had assured me, but not pretty or wardrobe-inclusive. "That was magic. You're . . ."

My uncle, Bradley, probably Ruby, possibly Ian and Jerome—that I knew of.

Bradley kissed my throat. "We're the real McCoys, and, baby, so are you."

Dragons and Dungeons

*Y*ou sold me out." I crossed my arms over my breasts and brought my knees up to meet them. Making myself a smaller target, hyperaware of Bradley so close by my side. He and Ruby, they were one thing. But Uncle D had been family. At least, he used to be. His official status might've been undead, but he was totally dead to me.

"No, honey, I offered you for blessing. It was best for everyone. You were, you and that boy . . ." My uncle retreated to the stairs, one hand on the rail. "That beast."

I felt a rush of relief, knowing Kieren wasn't in it with them. Then I realized that they'd been poisoning me against him for some time, and my faith hadn't been strong enough to see through it. I'd failed the last person left in this world that I still loved.

Kieren had been right all along. The vampires, these vampires, were killers.

I closed my eyes against the memory of Vaggio's murder, his neck ripped out. The claw marks. By taking wolf form and killing him, they'd created an opening for Bradley at Sanguini's, pointed my suspicion toward Kieren—mine and the police's. That night, Bradley himself might've been conveniently cooking at Chat Lunatique, but that didn't mean he hadn't masterminded the whole thing. Or maybe it *had* been Bradley, and the restaurant manager in Paris, Texas, was yet another vampire who'd lied on his behalf. As far as I was concerned, they were all monsters, all equally to blame.

"Just think," Uncle D added, turning back to look at me, "if I'd been blessed a few years earlier, I could've blessed your parents in turn."

"Blessed?" I repeated.

"And they would—"

"Still be dead."

"Still be with us. Don't you see? This way we never have to lose each other like we did them. That is our blessing. This way we can rebuild our family and it'll last."

It was sad, but he'd clearly gone stark, raving Looney Tunes. I clamped my chattering teeth together to still them.

"You'll thank me. You'll see." With that, Uncle D went upstairs.

Now, it was just the two of us. Me and the vampire chef.

"You never bit me," I whispered, raising my hand to my neck.

Bradley slid his tongue along my throat. "It's not the bite —"

"It's the blood." I remembered now.

Bradley hadn't just slipped something into my wine, he'd slipped *something* into my wine. But not just the wine, not necessarily. My mind clicked through the predator menu. Blood and tongue sausages with new potatoes, rice pudding blood cakes, veal tartare. For all I knew, Bradley had been dosing me since that first bowl of rigatoni marinara. It had been about a month since Bradley had entered my life. Long enough to transform me.

"Sir," grunted a voice from the top of the stairs. Jerome's or Ian's.

"Ah, yes," Bradley mused. "Time to get to work."

He left. The door at the top of the stairs shut, and I heard a bolt slide into place.

Then it was like the dangly bare bulb hanging from the ceiling flashed over my head. Three, five vampires? How often did they feed? I thought of the murdered, the missing. Where were the rest of the bodies? My gaze drifted to the crawl space. It was dark and narrow and somehow I could see inside anyway.

The space was empty except for spiders and a few mice that scurried to the far back, apparently sensing me, then huddled, black eyes wide. I could hear seven tiny hearts clicking. I couldn't reach them, didn't know why they were so afraid.

A few hours later, Ruby moseyed down. Her expression was guarded, gauging mine.

"Is, is Bradley turning everyone at Sanguini's into a vampire?" I asked. Not perfect, but under the circumstances, I took comfort in how brave I'd sounded. If I were to have any hope of freeing myself, I had to somehow keep a level head.

Ruby crouched on the bottom stair, eyeing me before creeping closer. As she approached the bare bulb, her pupils narrowed. She raised her hand to her mouth and licked the back of it. "Why? What have you heard?"

Licked off blood, I realized, unsure I wanted to know who or what had been on the menu. I'd had cravings before, for salty fries or chocolate ice cream, like clockwork for three days a month. Nothing. *Nothing* compared to this. I wanted to run my tongue where hers had been, flick it between her fingers, suck on her thumb. I didn't feel as afraid anymore.

"Tell me," she insisted from the center of the room. "Did the boss fill you in?"

"Bradley?" I shook my head. "He had to go to work."

"I suppose you'll find out sooner or later. No, not everyone. The most bloodthirsty, the most daring, those best suited to become vampires. The ones who ordered the chilled baby squirrels."

Simmered in orange brandy, bathed in honey cream sauce.

"Is it still Sunday?" I asked.

Ruby arched her back, posing. "Yeah, so?"

Day of rest. "So when he said he had to go to work . . . ?"

"Don't know," she replied. "They don't tell me everything yet."

Because she wasn't quite a vampire, I realized, fighting not to think about the full ramifications of what they'd done to me.

It was Sunday. Sanguini's was closed. But we'd already served about one hundred and fifty guests, and some of the staff had tried the squirrels, too. Yani, Mercedes, Sergio, the mayor, the *Tejano Food Life* critic, the woman who couldn't pee in a room with a man. Little Nathaniel. Not all of the customers, though. Not the ones who picked the prey menu or the blood cakes or skipped dessert.

"What about the murders, the ones at the lake?"

Her smile was all Cheshire. "Could've been one of them, could've been a rogue.

"By undead standards, Bradley has always been ambitious, impatient. But he's also a romantic who loves to cook and has always wanted a comfortable plot to call home. Complete with the little missus. Vampire subdivision. Vampire PTA."

Ruby stretched her arms above her head, apparently bored. "Plus, becoming a family man has inspired him to new heights." She explained that vampires traditionally chose their fledglings carefully, keeping numbers low, the ranks controllable. That they took the long view, building a power base over generations. But unwilling to wait, Bradley had embarked on his so-called "mass-blessing" plan. He'd seek out his soon-to-manifest neophytes, flex some muscle to show them who's boss, run a series of crash courses in Undead 101, and send off his most promising to claim Houston, Dallas, Fort Worth, San Antonio, El Paso, Corpus Christi—the other major Texas cities—in his name. "In a few months," she concluded, "he'll control the entire state."

"And me?" I asked. "What about—"

"My, aren't you self-absorbed," she said.

Pillow Talk

*W*hen I woke up, the room was pitch-black. I could feel a man beside me, a coppery velvet on my tongue. My palm rested on his broad forehead, and the hair felt silky. I remembered hearing somewhere that after you died, your hair and nails kept growing. I wondered if vampires had some kind of special conditioner. One that "brings your hair back to life." That got me giggling, giddy. I was drunk again.

"I hated having to do this, locking you down here," Bradley whispered, and his breath smelled like peppermint, blood, and Chianti. "But your vampiric attributes are beginning to manifest. Now that you're coming to terms with it, I'm going to free you. Just be careful. A wrong move could put you in grave danger."

Very punny, I thought. *Grave* danger. "What do you mean?"

"As a neophyte, you'll be vulnerable—erratic and exposed." Bradley traced lazy circles on my back. "Humans are no problem. At best, recruits. At least, food. But the werecarnivores, they're prey with teeth of their own. Can't be turned, and they tend to take it personally when you eat one. Some of the monsters even presume to spy on us, to hunt and assassinate us. They seek to foil our well-laid plans.

"Stay wary until your first tooth-to-skin feed. I don't want to lose you."

I was a little curious. "Lose me how?"

Bradley's fingers paused. "Wooden stake through the heart, head cut off. Mouth stuffed with garlic, if someone truly cares."

I shuddered.

"All of that isn't required. Decapitation will suffice or a knife, any knife, to the heart." Bradley kissed me, and I felt it dirty my toenails.

"There are other fatal dangers, like fire, and turnoffs, like sunlight, which reduce our powers. The effects of religious symbols vary from symbol to symbol and vampire to vampire. But the full treatment with the garlic, that's what the beasts think it takes to save our souls. Most don't bother."

Kieren was traditional about all that Wolf stuff.

"Tomorrow night, take off work. Think about what you want for the rest of your eternal life, and then meet me after close on Sanguini's dance floor." He lowered his voice. "Bring a beverage, why don't you? A token of affection."

A victim, he meant.

"And tell me you'll be forever mine."

My eyelids felt like canvas. My muscles, like gelatin. Not far away, a train whistle blew. It reminded me of Kieren. "And if I don't?"

"My little rebel." Bradley laughed. "You're the bee's knees." He slid his hand down the back of my thigh. "Without my guidance, my protection, the mongrel will become a menace to you. I'll have no choice but to put him down."

I made a small sound of alarm.

Bradley pulled one of my bee's knees over his slender hip. "When all's done, he won't matter. The blood will take away your loneliness, your fears. The success of Sanguini's will be guaranteed, and you'll always have me."

He made it sound so easy.

Bradley slid his palm back up. "You know, baby, the young people used to say 'necking' instead of 'kissing.'"

Which was interesting enough, cool and cozy. I could hear the bedsprings creaking, the beating hearts of the mice, my breath—hollow and wild. Feel my fading pulse in my muscles—the long ones and the bunched ones—my tendons, my toes, and my clenching, unclenching, clenching hands. Sweat broke out behind my knees, shimmered across my back. I shut my eyes against my need and his. Bradley slid lower, trailing wet kisses, heightening, heating, and then all I knew was the bite, the bliss, rapture.

dolce

Baby Got Bite

Grackles outside my bedroom window woke me from my recurring standardized-test nightmare, the one where I found out with a minute to go that I'd skipped a row of bubbles, so at most I'd have to retest and at least offer up prayers to the goddess of chaos.

I opened one eye, reassured by the familiar calico print of the bedspread covering my canopy bed, grateful Vaggio had sprung for the kajillion-thread-count sheets he'd given me last Christmas. Downstairs, the grandfather clock bonged.

I stilled, remembering Bradley's threat and expectations.

Kieren.

If I didn't bring Bradley a victim tonight and pledge my undead devotion, he would kill Kieren. And even if I did meet his terms, I didn't trust him.

It was like Miz Morales had said. Kieren needed the protection of a Wolf pack.

Meanwhile, I couldn't fall apart. Not while his life might depend on me.

Grabbing the phone on my nightstand, I tried Kieren at home, wishing Miz Morales had never taken his cell away. No answer, but my dial tone was beeping to signal messages. I checked Call Notes. Eleven new.

Yesterday morning, 9:28 A.M. "Quince? This is Kieren. I thought maybe you might be hurtin' this morning. Too much to drink, huh? Look, forget last night. I was upset. I'd love to talk to you once you've sobered up. Give me a call."

Another. Yesterday afternoon, 3:16 P.M. "Quince, I'm calling from Clyde's cell. I'll be at your place in a few."

Another. Last night, 8:16 P.M. "Quince, it's me. I'm outside your back door. This is the fourth time I've swung by, and it still doesn't look like anyone's home."

And so on, through the night, each more frantic. He'd called from outside Sanguini's, Ruby's apartment, tried my house a couple more times, mentioned using a pay phone, said something about his mama and daddy.

Message eight at 5:49 A.M. this morning began, "I tracked down an address on the vampire chef, and I'm headed north on Lamar."

I held my breath, praying, until message nine at 7:11 A.M. reported, "The only ones there were his goons." Ian and Jerome. "I've got a lead at school," Kieren went on. "Quince, if you get this message, I . . . I swear, I'm gonna find you."

Message ten at 2:43 P.M. "Something's going down," he said. "If you don't hear from me again, I just want you to know that I—sorry, I gotta go." And that was it.

Message eleven at 6:30 P.M. Bradley. "Good evening, baby. Sleep well?"

I dropped the phone like it was a rattler. Then picked it up and left a message at Kieren's.

Was it Monday? My alarm clock read 8:21 P.M., and come to think of it, I wasn't sure if I was home alone. After all, I hadn't escaped. I'd been delivered. As had a dozen long-stem red calla lilies, arranged in a crystal vase that sat on my dresser.

I lay quiet for five minutes, ten, listening for all the sounds an old house makes. Separating those from the noise of the birds. The wind against the frame, the haunting groans I excused as "settling." No footsteps on the stairs, no water running, no creaks on the hardwood floors.

When I turned down my covers, I was still dressed in the gauzy white gown, untied at the bodice. Jaw tight, I peeked down at myself. Beige thong still on. Beige thong still intact. My breasts and tummy didn't look pale, though I wasn't what anyone would call a bronzed beauty. I slipped out of bed, pulled the gown over my head, let it fall to the rug.

I didn't feel like a vampire. I did feel naked, though, and corrected that in a hurry, ditching what Bradley had left me with and pulling on sensible black cotton panties, a sports bra, black capri-cut running pants, my Fat Lorenzo's T, and Teva sandals. I missed my Nikes. Wished I hadn't left my red cowboy boots at the restaurant.

While dressing, I discovered the marks. Twin holes, blood crusted over, healing already. One set beneath the under curve of each breast. Another just below the navel, a fourth on my right inner thigh, the last behind my left kneecap. God damn him!

Bradley hadn't fed. Or drunk. He'd tasted. When

I touched the marks, teased them with my fingertips, peeled back the scab beneath my belly button, letting the blood run, I tasted myself. I tasted, and, trembling, wanted more.

The ritual of dressing had calmed me enough that I could think about searching the house. Not too calm, though. I wasn't too calm. I almost felt like Bradley could see me, or at least that he could anticipate my next move.

I peered at the dust bunnies beneath my bed, into the messy closet. All clear.

I took cautious steps to Uncle Davidson's room down the hall. Empty.

Small balcony outside the sliding glass door, also empty.

Back inside, it was a typical bachelor's room. Nondescript brown-and-gold striped bedding. Mismatched furniture, '50s stuff. A red lily in a vase on the dresser.

I rummaged. Lots of Hawaiian shirts, boxers, cutoff jeans. Not that it mattered, but Uncle Davidson hadn't given Ruby a drawer.

I wasn't sure what I was looking for until I found it in the top of the nightstand. Along with the strawberry-flavored condoms and the blindfold and cheap handcuffs, I discovered a box labeled ".45 Colt Silver

Bullets." In the next drawer down, I discovered Grampa Crimi's gun. The thief had been Uncle D.

Was I a gun person? Hell no, I was *not* a gun person. I was a desperate, on-a-life-or-death-deadline person. No, worse, I supposedly wasn't even a person. Not anymore.

The antique Colt Peacemaker was worth a fortune, which was why my peacenik parents had never gotten rid of it. A gift to Grampa from a fellow Marine whose life he'd saved in Korea. Like the restaurant, it was part of my family legacy.

I took the gun and the ammo box, knowing better than to leave them for my uncle.

Moving on, I saw the master suite was vacant, though a single red lily rested in a bud vase on the chest of drawers. I kept reminding myself not to hurry so much that I missed something. I leaped into the master bath, unloaded gun drawn. Empty.

Glancing at my reflection in the mirror, I froze like I'd been struck by rigor mortis.

Lacking a better idea, I closed my eyes, counted to ten, and then looked again.

Fangs, red eyes, pale skin, pointy long nails, my hair curly and clean. Had it been washed by Bradley himself? Ruby and my uncle? Ian and Jerome? That had been a violation, too, the way they'd treated me like a cadaver. Not that the hair was what mattered. Not like the thing staring back. Another vampire.

It was real. It was monstrous.

And it was *me*.

Dental Care

*T*he word "corpse" crossed my mind, and I hated how it sounded.

I remembered having seen Bradley look perfectly human once, that evening we'd met. Plus, Uncle Davidson had passed as human with beachcomber aplomb. And so far, Ruby had confined her Princess of Darkness persona to hair, makeup, and wardrobe.

Did they get manicures? I wondered. Flesh-colored base?

In the medicine cabinet, I found clippers and cut each of my pointy nails, wondering if it was one of those mind-matter scenarios. This time when I closed my eyes I tried to achieve some sense of inner tranquility. I wished I knew a calming chant or happened to be a Catholic, what with the self-crossing. Some thing ritualistic seemed appropriate, and Mama had been Catholic before she got married. But I was still me. Sort of. So after saying a simple Protestant prayer, I opened them again.

No luck. Maybe God didn't listen to vampires.

I grimaced and noticed that my teeth, fangs, had been stained with wine, blood.

Reaching back into the cabinet, I pulled out a long-forgotten box of baking soda. Daddy had been an occasional red wine drinker, and every once in a while he used to brush his teeth with baking soda to clean them.

I tore open a toothbrush package, a freebie from the dentist, wet the bristles, and dipped it into the gold box. The baking soda felt grainy and tasted medicinal. I scrubbed hard, harder, losing bristles between my teeth and fangs. Licked the blood from my gums. Filled a Dixie cup with water, swished it around, and spat. Grabbed some floss and ground it into the tender crevices until the bristles were gone.

My teeth were still brownish.

Frustrated, I tossed the barren toothbrush handle at the mirror, and it shot back. I caught it on reflex, one-handed. Threw it again, using more muscle. And again, I snatched it from the air without effort. Once more, grabbing the handle before it hit the sink. Flexing, I snapped the plastic. Damn.

I punched my reflection, the break spreading like a spiderweb. Now, the image looked more the way I felt. Uglier, fragmented, surreal.

My fangs ached, too, like first-day braces after the Novocain wore off.

ANGEL MIA

I checked my reflection again in the bathroom across the hall from my room. Same scary, though I could reflect. What else was just mythology? What wasn't?

Sunlight hadn't seemed to fry Uncle D or Bradley, confirming what Kieren had said about that supposed weakness being wishful thinking on the part of nervous humans. I recalled Bradley mentioning something about it reducing powers, which begged the question of what powers he was talking about. I tried to take my pulse at the wrist, the neck, and came up empty. Though Uncle D had seemed to manage church okay, I wasn't about to experiment with the holy-water-washed windows—courtesy of Clyde and Travis—in my bedroom or the Bible on my parents' nightstand. I kept moving.

Downstairs, I inspected the family and living rooms. Peering, peeking, moving pillows, raising cushions. Falling to my knees to look under furniture. Lily on the mantel, another on the coffee table, the dining room table, the TV cabinet.

I pushed back to my feet, and that's when the pain hit. Sharp, brutal, strong enough to make me salivate. Like something with claws had jammed them into my gut and decided to stir. Enjoyed stirring.

It was worth it, though, because suddenly I could feel again. I could feel *everything*—the grief, the fear, the remorse and betrayal, the mortification. The shame and love and worry. I could feel in my heart, my bowels, in the marrow of my bones, and the soft tissue of my organs. I was more *me* once more. Not the drunken, mood-swinging substitute that had been erratically taking over since Bradley had first arrived.

In the downstairs bath, another lily. I wiped away a reddish tear.

The *Cap City News* beside the lily on the kitchen island was dated Monday, September 16. Another unidentified body had been found near the lake. That was the—what?—third murder since Vaggio's that the police knew of. And—God!—neighbors had been asked to alert police if they noticed any suspicious persons or canines.

Bradley had been clever. If he didn't take out the competition, there was always APD. That reminded me, since Saturday night, had Uncle D called the cops? Maybe not. My uncle wouldn't have wanted the police digging for phone records to investigate the call moments before Vaggio's death. Especially since it was him or Bradley or one of them who'd . . .

It might be too late for Vaggio, but hopefully, Kieren was still alive.

On my wildflowers calendar hanging from the side of the fridge, Tuesday, September 17, had been circled in red ink. Two A.M. was scrawled in the square.

I'd tried to be thorough searching the house, so it had taken over an hour. I had four and a half left, give or take, before I was due at Sanguini's with a victim. Or else.

I left two more messages on the Morales answering system (the home line and Miz Morales's business number) for Kieren to call my cell.

Then I found my student directory in the drawer nearest the kitchen phone and left a message for him at Clyde's, too.

My laptop was on the table. Within seconds I'd already tried and failed to IM Kieren and was logging on to my e-mail account. He'd sent thirty-some messages. One each time he'd found some reference to Bradley in his research. A few just pleading for me to believe him. Nothing new, though, since yesterday. I hit REPLY to the latest and kept it brief. Apologized. Told him to vamoose. Said if he had to talk first to call my cell. Typed *Love You*. Erased it. Hit SEND.

I deleted everything in my SENT folder, then everything in my TRASH folder.

At something of a loss, I realized I hadn't eaten in a couple of days and checked the refrigerator. Low blood sugar, fatigue, and cutting my teeth had taken a lot out of me.

The refrigerator was mostly empty. I'd been dining at the restaurant, eating less and less the past few days, and unless I missed my guess, Uncle Davidson had been on a liquid diet for quite a while. Speaking of which, I snagged the half-empty bottle of Chianti from the top shelf. The label read "Sanguini's: A Very Rare Restaurant."

The wine had soothed. Then the blood had transformed. But now I *had* to give it up, face the realities I'd been trying to drown.

A few twists of the cork later, I poured the thick red liquid down the drain. It chugged from the bottle, clung to the stainless steel. Flipping on the water to rinse, I fought the urge to inhale. Quitting cold turkey would be a bitch.

Trying to stay as positive as possible, I focused on my available choices. A half-empty package of hard salami, a container of cottage cheese that had expired two weeks ago, a bowl of diced red onion covered with fuzzy white mold, and a full bottle of Seltzer water. The cabinets were down to coffee filters, salt, a couple of cans of soup, a box of instant cocoa, and saltines. I checked the freezer and found a package of chicken legs dated five months earlier. I tried a cracker, and the salt was nice. But the texture scraped at my gag reflex, so I choked down some Seltzer, which came back up. The sink was handy, and some blood spilled out with the rest. I shut my eyes against the glory of it.

DEAD WOMAN RUNNING

*M*y cell phone charge was dead, so I used the house phone to leave one more message with the Moraleses, saying that I was on my way.

It should've been a less than ten-minute run to Kieren's, even if I had to wait for the WALK sign. But I wasn't running, not yet. Every time my brain urged my feet to hurry, something distracted me. Mosquitoes on my skin, moisture in the air, the cat lounging on a front step. Fur bristling, he rolled to his paws and darted to the side, jumping behind a bush.

I spotted an old lady in her picture window, pulling the lace drapes closed. She was shrunken, shoulders bowed. I could hear her dogs barking from inside.

Two houses south, a family parked and climbed out of a BMW, a mama and daddy with their son. They looked healthy, blue-eyed blonds, practically translucent skin. He had to be about my age, the boy, though I didn't recognize him from school. Tourists maybe, or some suburban family out for a night on the wild side. The kind of people well networked into society.

I walked at a brisk pace, turned to cruise down the steep hill. Just ahead, a couple of girls were talking in sign language. They were cute, vibrant and juicy, with shiny black hair and a bounce in their steps. At the intersection, they turned off, heading north.

I ran the rest of the way. I wasn't sweating, though the humidity raised the hair on my arms. Wasn't breathing; I didn't have to. I slowed alongside a house with ducks and fancy chickens prancing in the backyard, had an unwelcome image of picking feathers out from between my teeth and fangs. At the Moraleses', Kieren's truck was parked in the driveway, but his mama's wedding planner van was gone.

"Kieren!" No one answered the bell; no one answered when I pounded on the front door. "Kieren!" I ran around the house, dodging Meghan's oversize red plastic wagon and the smaller antique metal one that Miz Morales used as a marigold planter.

Brazos's blue bandanna hung in tribute from a nail on his doghouse.

"Kieren!" I called, pounding at the back door. "Kieren!" I pounded until my knuckles bruised and bled. Pounded until my voice strained, until I was convinced the chittering cicadas were mocking me.

Unable to resist, I flattened my hands against the white door. Leaned in. Licked. The silky warmth delighted my tongue, and for a moment, I was somewhere else. Somewhere safe and salty and munchable down to my girl parts. Determined to suckle every last drop. That's when the door opened, and Meghan stood on the other side in her footie pajamas.

"Hi, Quincie." She should've been in her wicker bedroom, snuggled beneath her waffle-weave blanket with Otto the stuffed rabbit and Pet Doctor Barbie. It was past her bedtime. "You look funny."

I could only imagine.

"Did you hurt yourself?" she asked.

"Where's Kieren?"

"Not home. Papa's here."

Roberto. "Can I talk to him?"

Meghan jostled curly pigtails. "He's in the shower. I was watching the Cartoon Channel, but it's not funny tonight."

No, nothing was funny tonight.

"You smell funny, too."

Dead. Did I smell dead? She smelled scrumptious.

"Close the door," I told Meghan.

Wide eyebrows met, puzzled and far too trusting. The change of expression shifted her scar, made her look broken, breakable.

"Close the goddamn door!"

She did. Slammed it shut against me.

Smart kid.

I put my hands back, fingers spread, where they had been and bent my head to lick again. When my knuckles were wet and clean, my brain shut down, and my body went on autopilot. I needed more. More blood. Now.

Back around the house to Kieren's truck. Locked, but that didn't matter with the windows rolled down, spare key where it always was, in the ashtray. I was losing, I realized. Losing myself.

Lost.

"Nightwing"

It took only minutes to reach Town Lake, park Kieren's truck, and join the crowd gathered beneath the Congress Avenue Bridge.

Too many people, I thought. Too close together, too obvious. A much-tattooed woman glanced at my face and drew her boyfriend closer, slid her hand in the back pocket of his jeans. A couple of gym-buffed boys looked my way, too, but they appeared happy enough with each other, and, besides, they were too young. Too strong. The cop hovering behind the Bat Anti-Defamation League table stood with his arms folded across his chest, somehow managing to seem bored and attentive. The crowd of tourists and locals was lighter than it used to be before the murders. Bats flitted out, one after another from beneath the bridge, ravenous, but the main exodus was over.

I skirted the edge of the thinning group and then inched down the broad, sandy path, uncomfortable around the water, peering into the lush growth. I strayed off the trail here and there, listening for I wasn't sure what. My hearing was much improved, my night vision even better. Between blowing leaves, a dragonfly hovered over black ripples, exquisite, iridescent—then, with a crunch of rodent jaws, became food.

On a bench at the next dock, an old man lay sleeping. Cardboard was covering his face, neck, and shoulders. His chest was still, very. . . . But his foot was moving, jerking in its torn and filthy tennis shoe.

The dock creaked with my first step, but the man didn't awaken.

I looked around. No witnesses. These days, none of the eco-tourists or joggers would dare venture this far onto the trail.

A closer examination of the long-sleeve flannel

shirt and pajama bottoms confirmed it. He'd probably strolled down to watch the ducks and fell asleep.

I slid the cardboard aside, revealing Mitch's face. Stubbly, bloated by alcohol. The Santa-blue eyes closed, peaceful.

My gums ached, burned, bled. I moved in, licked my lips. Just a taste, or until I drowned, either way.

No one would miss Mitch, not for days. I could dump him here in the water. The perfect victim. Unloved. Just another body found at the lake. This was why Bradley had remade me. How could I resist?

My hair fell from my shoulders, grazing his face, and Mitch's hand shot out, palming my throat like a football. He opened his red eyes and, roaring, his mouth—sharp fangs and fingernails extending as the cardboard slipped to the dock. The fingers closed, crushing. Then he caught sight of my face, my eyes, my fangs. And released. His mouth dropping into an *O* of surprise and apology.

I coughed, realizing I wasn't the only one who'd been caught off-guard. Raising a hand to my neck, I felt the bleeding, V-shaped marks his nails had left. I'd been foolish, I realized, to cut mine. Bradley had fed Mitch when he'd stopped by the back door at the restaurant, I recalled, and weeks before that. Infected him.

"Oops, holy crap, Miss Missy. Quincie, girl, I didn't know you was a vampire, too." Mitch's eyes faded back to blue, and his fangs retracted.

I thought about saying I was sorry for trying to hurt him, for not being the meal he'd hoped, for his having died. I settled for "How'd you do that?"

He sat up, his head tilting, his expression as kind as ever. "Do?"

"Change back. Um, look human again."

"Haven't, you know, you taken a big bite, had your first yet?"

"No." Once again I was myself, in control and resolved to stay that way. I hoped I could stay that way.

What time was it? Ten? God, what if Kieren had tried to call me at home?

"Ah," Mitch patted my arm. "You, you gotta get the first one down so the brain, so it lets you go." He pointed to his head, as if to illustrate. "All that changing . . . You're a regular girl, oops! Got some good blood somewhere, in the tummy, in the veins, and now you're, you're improved and new. But the body, the sys, system, it thinks that way for a while, like a human, but then the feed, it takes over. It takes you, and you're all good. Once you get the first one. Being a vamp, vampire is all tied up, messed up with um, the, the—"

"Blood."

"Yep, almost. Nope, wait. Spoke too, too soon. Not just that. The feed, that's what it is. The bite. Once you get past that, you, you'll get more of a hold on it, Miss Quincie."

Was Mitch the one responsible for the lakefront murders?

I glanced at the hand-lettered cardboard at my feet. It read:

HOMELESS INDIE
PRO-LIFE VAMPIRE
NEEDS BLOOD

"Hocus-pocus," Mitch added. "Spooky me, spooky you."

HIGH PROTEIN, LOW CARB

*H*hair past 1 A.M. Tuesday morning. Kieren hadn't called me back. The longer I waited, the hungrier I got. The shock of Mitch had brought me back to myself, but it would be so easy to slip again. I hadn't even realized I'd been on the hunt until putting Kieren's truck into gear, and by then . . . Christ. *Meghan.*

I got up from my kitchen table, retraced my path back across the black-and-white checked tile, and opened the freezer door. Using my fingernail, I ripped open the plastic wrap, set two icy, stuck-together chicken legs on a plate, covered it with a paper towel, slid the plate into the microwave, and hit DEFROST.

I had just sworn off the sauce, so to speak, but humans consumed animal blood all the time. Hopefully, it didn't count. And I needed a fix. Quick.

As the microwave hummed, its interior tray turning, I paced, pausing to run my fingertips along the wall phone, to tangle them in the curly black plastic cord, repressing the urge to rip it out. Where was Kieren, anyway?

I had less than an hour.

The microwave beeped three times, and I removed my sustenance. Courtesy of modern technology, the pale, fleshy poultry legs lay in a pool of watery blood.

Arguing to myself that salmonella wasn't a burning vampire health concern, I dipped my finger in the liquid and raised it to my lips. The meat repulsed me, but I picked up a leg and licked it like a Popsicle.

The leg was mostly sucked dry when the doorbell rang.

Let it be Kieren, I prayed.

It was Detective Bartok and Detective Matthews.

Self-conscious, I hid my snack behind my back.

"We're looking for Kieren Morales," Detective Bartok said from the front step.

"I don't know where he is," I replied from the doorway, glad I'd parked the truck a few blocks southwest so Uncle D wouldn't see it. "Did my uncle call you?"

Matthews, the senior officer, shook his head. "We haven't talked to him since he came down to the station. Why? Does he have something to tell us?"

I stuck with the truth, so as to trigger their cop instincts as little as possible. "As far as I know, the last either of us talked to APD was when Detective Sanchez called me at Sanguini's on the third. I remember because it was ten days until the reopening."

They traded a look.

"And what did Detective Sanchez call regarding?" Bartok asked.

"Well, he said—"

"He?" Matthews interrupted.

I nodded, still hiding the chicken leg.

"We have only one Detective Sanchez on the force," Detective Bartok explained. "And she's the mother of three. What did this person say to you?"

I summarized, realizing the caller had likely been

following Bradley's orders. Planting suspicion. God, I was an idiot.

"You still have my card?" Detective Bartok asked. At my second nod, she went on. "Please give us a call if you hear from Mr. Morales, and if someone else claiming to be from the Austin Police Department contacts you, let us know immediately."

"Okay," I said. "Does, uh, Kieren know you're looking for him?" Was it only the vampires I needed to warn him about? I wondered. Or the police, too?

"We've left a lot of messages since yesterday," Detective Matthews said. "We just want to talk to him, that's all."

I didn't believe them. I thought they were ready to make an arrest. But they were nice people. They were trying to serve and protect, to do what they thought needed to be done. For a split second I considered telling them everything I knew. But what if they didn't believe me? What if my talking somehow made things worse?

"Nice vampire makeup, by the way," Detective Bartok added. "Very professional. Like in the movies or something."

I'd almost forgotten how I looked.

"The restaurant's apparently a real success,"

Detective Matthews pitched in. "I used to go there back when it was Fat Lorenzo's. Best lasagna in the world."

My dead heart sank. I said good-bye, shut the front door, and tossed the rest of the meat into the trash.

Cat and Louse

Uncle Davidson and Ruby walked in the back door, if you could call it walking in. They sort of stumbled, kissing, groping, across the kitchen. High on life, on blood, on love or whatever passed for it.

Arm in arm, they swayed on the tile.

"Shouldn't you be out hunting, honey?" my uncle asked.

Ruby trailed a finger down his throat, tracing the plump flowers on his Hawaiian shirt. "She's just a little girl. You wait here, Quincie. We won't take long—"

"Now, now," my uncle protested, laughing. "We'll see about that."

Vibrant, fed. Both of them. On something heartier than chicken. I wondered if they'd shown up at all for the Sanguini's dinner shift.

Ruby was wearing one of her damsel-of-the-damned getups, though she'd covered up with a short leather jacket that bordered on tasteful. "You bad, bad man. We have a family obligation." She chuckled. "We'll go hunting with you later, love. We're full now anyway."

I had to ask. "You killed somebody, didn't you?"

"Some bodies," Uncle D replied, beaming at Ruby.

"Your friends with the shiny badges," she clarified. "We ran into them on their way back to their car." Ruby glanced at my uncle, mock ashamed. "He'd wanted to bend their ears about your dog-face boy, but—"

"You ate the police?!" I exclaimed.

"Blood lust plus opportunity," Uncle D said. "Her teeth came in so fast. In the dark, I hardly spotted a flash of fang."

Ruby had already adapted. Killed, drunk, and put her human face back on. Quite the overachiever, I thought. It was what she'd always wanted, though.

"Relax," she said. "We got rid of the bodies. No one's going to find drained cops in the front yard."

My uncle shot her a reprimanding look. "But the boss won't approve."

"It's not like there aren't more police where those came from." Ruby licked her black lips. "APD is already looking for the Wolf. Now, they'll just assume he's a cop killer, too. I don't see where Bradley has much room to whine."

With that, Ruby pulled Uncle D out of the room, down the hall, and up the stairs. They were moaning before they reached the top, shuffling into his bedroom.

I hoped when he dug into the nightstand drawer for the strawberry-flavored condoms . . . if he'd . . . Did vampires need to worry about disease or birth control? Anyway, if Uncle D opened the drawer, I hoped that he'd be too preoccupied to miss the silver bullets I'd swiped earlier.

Given that I still hadn't heard from Kieren, I had to go it alone. Destroy the monsters that were a threat to him, hope he made it to the Wolf pack before the police found his trail. It was awful, but in a way, Ruby had done Kieren a favor. It would take awhile for APD to realize their detectives were missing, to send another team out after Kieren. If nothing else, she'd bought him some time.

I slunk into the family room, touched the jar of seashells Daddy had collected a lifetime earlier, whispered an apology. Then I reached behind the nearest throw pillow on the sofa and curled my palm around the butt of Grampa Crimi's gun.

THE SILVER BULLET

*A*t the kitchen table, I logged on to the Web. Turned out there was one correct way to load a Colt Peacemaker. You were supposed to slide in five bullets and then put the hammer down on the empty chamber. It was sort of an old-fashioned safety, so the gun wouldn't go off accidentally. If you wanted to shoot it, though, you had to cock the hammer each time. That's what it meant to call a gun "single action."

Being that they were vampires, the gun wouldn't destroy Ruby and Uncle Davidson. I got that. But if I were lucky, a silver bullet would put them out of commission until I had a chance to confront Bradley, who'd be left with only Ian and Jerome. And since they'd sacrificed me, I thought I could pull the trigger. I was ready to call on my inner vampire if that's what it took to get the job done.

I waited through the gasps, mews, and an unexpected cracking noise until the grandfather clock in the hall chimed a quarter till two. Then I hurried up the stairs and found Uncle D's door slightly open. I slipped into the room, shameless, the gun drawn in front of me, expecting to see the lovers naked and undulating.

Instead, Uncle Davidson was lying on his stomach, face-down on the bed, a wooden stake protruding from his bleeding back. His neck was raw, too, turned as if the spinal cord had been severed. But that wasn't the most remarkable thing.

It was Ruby's body, her face, covered in shiny black fur, long whiskers sprouting from her cheeks. I'd, I'd *known* there was something weird about her!

Mesmerized, I tightened my grip and watched her finish—changing? shifting?—*shifting* into a werecat. The bones broke, rearranging and reknitting. The fur, the transformation, it was like watching slow-motion photography.

She was dazzling, with long, slinky muscles beneath the bristling fur. Soaking wet. All black except the Morticia streak, which had receded to an unnatural white splotch above her right ear. About five feet long from nose to haunches. Sniffing my uncle, lowering her muzzle to lick the blood streaming down his spine, running down either side of his back and into his armpits.

"What the—?" I whispered.

Ruby glared at me, and she tensed as if to spring.

"Nice kitty," I breathed. "Pretty kitty."

Double-O kitty, I realized. A spy.

Kieren hadn't told me much about the various species of werepeople—Cats included—except that they couldn't be trusted and liked to play with their food. That they were to be avoided in French kissing, as those with the best control could trigger the kind of wet tongue combs that in domestic kitties created a sandpaper effect and in wild cats could rip raw flesh from bone. That like the Wolves, they were distantly related to a long-forgotten Ice Age cousin. And like the Wolves, they were sworn enemies of vampires.

"Silver bullets," I said, hoping the specificity of the threat would make her take me more seriously. "I don't want to shoot you. But I will to defend myself. There's someplace I've got to be soon, *really* soon. Kieren's life is on the line."

Ruby yawned in reply. Huge, dramatic, as only a Cat could yawn.

If she had known about the baby squirrels for only a day or two, I wondered, had she told the Cats about Bradley? Probably not. She and Uncle D had been inseparable, and she'd *just* ditched him. I wouldn't stare at the body, the blood. I. Would. Stop. Staring.

Knowing what Uncle Davidson had become, his betrayal . . . It all went a long way toward squelching a lifetime of loving him. But I had still loved him for a lifetime.

No matter. If I failed tonight, maybe Ruby and the Cats could still stop Bradley. Not that she'd ever believe we were on the same side. "Go," I told her, stepping aside. "Leave now, and I'll let you pass unharmed."

Ruby's back arched, her tail thrashing.

"Go!" I shouted, cocking the hammer.

Her ears rotated.

I hoped that was a good sign.

It wasn't.

Ruby sprang at me, claws eager, her teeth gleaming like bloody knives. Furious. Fearless. Like she knew I'd never pull the trigger.

She was wrong. The shot was *loud*. Ruby dropped to the floor. The impact—heart, shoulder?—I couldn't tell, too much blood. For a moment, I was at a loss.

Then Ruby rose, bleeding. Far more pissed off than before I'd shot her. I aimed the gun once more.

"You know where Kieren lives," I said, trying reason. "You know his mama is a Wolf. She's also a healer. If you go to her, tonight, now, she'll help you." At least I thought she would. "The Cats are counting on you, aren't they? What good will it do if you get yourself killed?"

Ruby hesitated. Then she sprang again, only this time across the room and into the hallway. I heard her escape down the stairs and then a crash as though she'd broken through the back door.

"Good luck," I whispered, lowering the gun.

I had to move fast. Bradley was waiting.

It was messy, intoxicating, as I yanked the stained stake out of my uncle's back. I closed my hand on the wood, recognizing it as the thin handle of one of Bradley's black cherry cooking utensils. A ladle maybe, with the end broken off. I swept Ruby's discarded leather jacket up from the pile of her clothes on the floor, and my heightened hearing picked up sirens in the distance, closing in.

When I opened the sliding glass door to the balcony, the gun slipped through my fingers, fell, *thunked*. I left it behind, still gripping the stake in my other hand, tucking the jacket over my arm, and leaped from the second floor.

Would I break a leg, my neck? I wondered in midair, wishing I were an old enough vampire to turn into a bat.

I landed, rolling, absorbing the impact.

Go, I thought. Go, go, *go*.

HEARTS AT STAKE

*M*iz Morales's white minivan was parked on the street outside my house. Clyde was staring into the darkness from the passenger side. I crept up from behind, staying low against the logo that read *Endless Love Bridal Planning,* and opened the driver's door. Slid in fast, grabbed him. Thrilled that the key was in the ignition. It was 2:04 A.M., according to the dashboard clock, and Bradley wasn't known for his patience.

"Where's Kieren?" I demanded.

"You're a vampire!" Clyde exclaimed, hissing.

As if a vampire who'd already faced down a were-cat would be intimidated by a 'possum. "Where's Kieren?" I repeated.

"He, he took off after Ruby."

I turned on the ignition, released the emergency brake, and pulled from the curb.

Clyde was quiet until we passed the Capitol Motel. Then he asked, "What're you going to do with me?"

My on-the-fly plan was simple. Bradley expected me with "beverage" in tow. I'd bring Clyde. I'd play along, hand Clyde over to Bradley, and when Bradley lost himself in the blood lust, I'd stake him through the back like Ruby had staked Uncle D.

All this would happen before Clyde was sucked dry. Before Ian and Jerome, who hung out in the back lot until two thirty, came to Bradley's rescue. Hopefully.

Then all Kieren would have to worry about was the cops.

First, though, I needed to get Clyde's cooperation. I pulled the van into a spot on South Congress and parked. "I'm going to destroy Bradley. I am. But he's older than me and much more powerful. We need to catch him off-guard."

"We?!" Clyde's right hand fell to the door handle, and I gripped his left arm to hold him in place. White fur rolled across his face, his neck. The air in the van soured like rotten eggs. "*Wait,* I get it! You're going to sacrifice me to the master vampire!"

"I am not."

"You are *so!*" Chin folding into nose, nostrils in spasm. "You're going to—"

"No! My God, stop that."

"Stop what?" His voice was garbled, snout protruding.

Pressing a button to lower the driver's side window, I answered, "*That* that. With the sniffing and the . . . Yuck, what used to be your hands. Stop. I've got a plan." Sort of. "And this . . ." I gestured. "Is not part of it. So, shift back all the way. Now!"

The long whiskers shook. "I'm *trying,* okay?"

It was 2:09 A.M. now.

"Try *harder.*"

"Calm down. It's not like you're helping. I'm a guy, you know, hormones. And you're scary and sexy. In a gonna-kill-somebody kind of way."

"Sexy?" Somehow I doubted that.

Clyde's nose widened. Hair receded. Stench thinned. "You weren't nearly this hot as a human."

Despite everything, I still had an ego. "Rodent."

"Marsupial." He reached into the glove compartment to retrieve some moist towelettes. Biting the corner of a package, he fished one out and wiped his face.

"Hear me out," I said to Clyde, glancing out the open window. The street crowd was thinning from the entertainment district, the noise dying down. "We—"

"We should wait for Kieren."

It dawned on me then that Clyde didn't know Kieren was a hybrid, didn't know he couldn't shift all the way or on cue. "It's midmonth. Low power."

Clyde looked like he'd give anything to crawl back into his mama's pouch. "Yeah, between midmonth, Kieren's allergies, and Ruby's cinnamon stink water, he didn't know she was a Cat until I told him."

If that's what he wanted to think, fine by me. But we couldn't sit here all night. I quickly summed up what I had in mind and added, "I won't let you die like Travis."

Clyde wrung pink hands. "Vampires didn't kill Travis. Ruby did."

"But, but Ruby's a wereperson," I whispered. Sure, she'd killed humans, but I'd think even she would draw the line somewhere.

"Uh-huh. Hungry kitty. Not all of us wag our tails

for werepeople power." He didn't sound happy about it. "The Cats don't get along with the Wolves, for example, and they eat whom they please."

That sounded like Ruby. She'd killed Matthews and Bartok in case it was her they were after, I realized, for having eaten Travis.

"Thing is," Clyde said, "we all hate vampires—no offense."

I didn't say anything.

"But if you want to take out the *dolce* demon," he added, "count me in."

My accomplice was out of his furry gourd. Or, especially for a wereopossum, really brave. I admired him.

All good except just as I was about to reach for the driver's side handle, Kieren ripped the door off its hinges.

Backlit by the streetlight, I couldn't make out the expression on his face. I turned my head away, not wanting him to see me like this—eyes red, fangs extended, dead.

I tried to tell him to leave, but before the words could come, he reached into the vehicle and yanked me out, shoving my back against the side of the van.

My gaze fell to the turquoise-and-silver crucifix hanging from his neck, and I flinched. Maybe I was unholy now, but I hadn't chosen this. It wasn't my fault.

I didn't have to go on this way.

"Kieren . . ." Reaching into the jacket pocket, I withdrew the wooden handle. Forget risking Clyde, I thought. If I were history, wouldn't Bradley leave Kieren alone? That was all that was left, wasn't it? For Kieren to plunge this stake into my heart.

"Quince." Kieren pulled me against him, away from the van, and growling low, tore the weapon from my scarred hand.

THIS SIDE OF HEAVEN

I braced, but the pain never came. Instead, Kieren crushed the stake into splinters and kissed me, his lengthening canines knocking against my extended fangs. I gave in, selfish, sweeping my tongue inside his jaws, forcing my hipbones to rattle against his, giving in to the urge to grind. Curling my fingers into his lush hair, I flattened against him, inhaling sweat and denim and danger and home. Finally mine.

Kieren growled again, deep enough that my lips felt the vibration, and I thanked God we had this moment. He was so warm, so alive. It was the third and best kiss of my life, which might not sound like much, but it was more than I'd ever imagined.

The squeal of tires prompted us to break away as Clyde—who'd scooted to the driver's side, tossed the van in reverse, and backed out of the space—was peeling out, heading south to safety. He'd waited for an opening, faked us out.

"First, you steal my truck," Kieren said as the taillights faded in the distance. "Now, he's stealing the van."

"You can have the truck back," I breathed. "But be careful. The police—"

"I know. I'm a wanted Wolf-man," he agreed, "and if I'm arrested. . . . I have to think of my mother, Meghan. I promised my parents that I would leave tonight. They think I'm already gone."

"Just go now," I begged. "Be safe."

But Kieren insisted on hearing my side of the story, which I sped through, ending with Bradley's demands, explaining the now defunct plan with Clyde.

"You could come away with me," he said. "Pretty soon you'll be able to change into a wolf—"

"But not *shift*," I said. What he was suggesting, it was a nice fantasy, one I hoped to revisit in my dreams. But I wouldn't be a real Wolf, a natural Wolf like him, just a vampire in wolf form. No pack would accept me, and Kieren needed not only their protection, but also the chance to live without having to hide half of who he was. He'd get that different, special life. The one he'd prepared for. The one he deserved.

It was more important than how much I'd miss him, than how much I loved him, than anything. Still, I wondered, did he love me?

"Besides," I reminded Kieren, "Bradley is using my restaurant to create new vampires. I'll torch the place before I let him go on doing that, but you—"

"I'm not leaving until you're free of that monster. He killed . . ."

Vaggio? I thought. Brazos?

Then I understood. Kieren had meant me. Me as Bradley's victim. Kieren just couldn't bring himself to say it. His tear tracks glittered blue and green from the neon sign overhead. He'd tried hard, so hard, to save me. He was still trying, even though in many ways it was too late.

Kieren did love me.

I cradled his stubbly wet cheek. "You can't—"

"Same plan," Kieren went on. He broke the silver chain from his neck, tossed the crucifix toward the empty lot next door. "Except I'm your 'victim' instead of Clyde."

"Um." I pointed at the splintered wood on the asphalt. "That was the plan."

"This is the new one. When he moves in to feed, I can take him. That time at the railroad tracks, it was my self-preservation instinct kicking in. It'll kick in again. Instead of that stake, I'll pretend to be a willing sacrifice and then surprise him with my claws."

I wasn't sure. "Do you think he'll fall for that? He knows what you are."

Kieren shrugged. "If he doesn't, he doesn't. You just stay out of the way."

He might as well have said "on the sidelines," but I'd never doubt Kieren again. "What about Bradley's bodyguards?"

Kieren slipped an arm through mine, escorting me around the discarded van door, toward Sanguini's, and tilted his head upward, leading my gaze to the roof of the restaurant, where the most enormous bird was perched. Make that "birds." Two. Red heads, dark wings lightly tipped. Must've been six feet long, must've had a sixteen-foot wingspan. They launched into the sky.

"Ian and Jerome," Kieren explained. "Turkey were-vultures. They eat carrion, and vampire leftovers are hearty. That's why drained bodies hardly ever show up in the news, just missing persons. Because of werescavengers. But I've talked to them, wereperson to wereperson. They won't interfere."

It sounded like he'd had a busy day. "Clyde told me that all werepeople hated vampires," I said, newly sensitive about the subject. And what was it Kieren himself had called us? Dead people too selfish to lie down? Damned?

"Nothing is that simple," he replied. "Not anymore."

I felt a spark of hope. "Us moseying in together, that's the last thing Bradley will expect. Until now, he's been running this whole show."

"Until now."

Turned out there was some big, bad Wolf in my good boy after all.

A Drinking Problem

*W*hen we walked past my family photo gallery, through the crimson velvet curtains, and into Sanguini's dining room, Bradley looked frazzled in the middle of the dance floor. He had honey cream sauce on his collar and blood on his tie. No cape.

It was the most real, the most human he'd seemed in days. No matter what he might be, what all he'd done, running a red-hot restaurant was brutal work. I felt less foolish for falling for the act.

Bradley studied my new vampiric features, how my face reflected what he'd done to me. I half expected him to gloat, but he looked pensive, reflective. His gaze flicked once, as if unconcerned, to Kieren. "Baby, you're late."

What was his hurry? The eternal who missed humanity so much that he fed it. Must've let the staff go at close, I realized. The tables were clean, sconces turned off, chandeliers shining. Calla lilies in vases on each table. I was willing to bet, though, that the kitchen was a disaster area. How many guests had tried the squirrels tonight?

"I brought the 'beverage' you asked for," I said.

"Pity you didn't select something with a lovelier bouquet. I'd hoped for a better vintage for your first. But I must admit, this gesture, it's a tremendous show of your *changing* loyalties. I'm touched." His next words were for Kieren. "Rough day at school? I hear somebody beheaded the vice principal."

I had to stiffen to keep my knees from buckling. There was only one reason Kieren would ever behead somebody.

Vice Principal Harding had been a vampire. He'd painted my locker, encouraged me to homeschool, because Waterloo High had been competition for

Bradley, another anchor to the human world. A place Kieren went five days a week.

"And now this," Bradley went on. "Sacrificing your life for Quincie. I'm impressed." He nodded my way. "Go ahead, baby. Ladies first."

Me? I thought. "You want *me* to bite *him*?"

THIS SIDE OF HELL

Without warning, Kieren threw his body forward to tackle Bradley, who changed in a flash into a red-eyed wolf, teeth bared, as if to pit one beast against another. But then Bradley dissolved into mist just as their bodies would've collided.

Kieren slammed into the dance floor, and I ran to kneel by his side.

Bradley reappeared in human form—fully clothed—where we had been standing. He laughed.

"It might've been a kick to see how things played out, but I hate the taste of Wolf and he's already taken out one vampire today. A novice, but still, I didn't get to be this old by taking chances."

Kieren radiated heat, energy, anger. I helped him back to his feet.

"Tell you what, baby," Bradley went on. "I'll make you a deal. A more interesting one. Drink. Drink your fill. And then *if* you somehow manage to tear yourself from his throat in time to save him, if after having drunk, he's still what you think you want, fine. I can bully you into obedience, but not love. Not the kind of freely given devotion I seek. At some point, you would have to *choose* to be mine. Say the word, and I'll back off, way off. *Adios. Addio.* Good-bye."

That was interesting, except . . . "Let me get this straight. You're saying you'll just give up? Leave me alone, let Kieren go? Do you think I'm that clueless?" I paused, too intent to be embarrassed. "I mean, now."

"Quince," Kieren began. "You can't negotiate with—"

"Think of the drama," Bradley replied, gesturing across the dining room. "That's what Sanguini's is all about, isn't it? What would be the point of letting you taste him, if the stakes weren't all or nothing? And besides, he was right about one thing. Wolves don't live that long, even less than the average human. I couldn't use him to keep you in line forever."

"You'll abandon Sanguini's," I pressed, making my terms clear. "Leave Austin, bats and all?"

"Why not?" Bradley replied, in a tone that suggested it would never come to that. "It's your restaurant, your city. I couldn't very well rule from here after letting you spurn me without first staking you, and romantic fool that I am, I doubt I could bring myself to do it." He paused. "San Antonio has better architecture anyway."

Bradley had already done so much damage. I thought of the loss, the chaos to come. "What about the squirrel eaters?" I asked. "The vamps-in-waiting?"

"Quince." Kieren again. "I—"

"Shut up, boy!" Bradley yelled, before returning his attention to me. He took a moment to center himself. "Consider the neophytes a parting gift."

How magnanimous. I clicked off the days in my mind. Mid-October. Happy Halloween to me.

Did I trust Bradley? No. Yes. *No,* I didn't trust him, but I did believe he meant what he'd said. I would get stronger. He'd told me as much in his parlor. *I needed for you to come to me.* He still did. Sooner or later, he'd need me to offer myself.

Freely and of my own will.

The dining room was heavy with expectation. It was time to get it on, but I just . . .

Bradley's laugh was carefree. "This is the most fun I've had in ages."

It was clear: he thought he'd won.

Turning to Kieren, I raised tentative fingers to his feverish neck, to curl in the wavy hair. Something wicked inside me welled up and whispered that I should dive in.

"Get it over with," Kieren rumbled. "Quince, get it over—" Just then, Kieren's self-preservation instinct came through. His goatee spread, eyebrows thickened, claws sprouted from shaking hands. "Quince!" His voice turned desperate. "Quince, *get back!*"

I felt frozen, mesmerized by his desire, his rage. His caged beast breaking free again. It was frustrated, confused, in pain. Eager to lash out. At anybody.

"Or," Bradley said, suddenly serious, "maybe I should kill him before he shreds you into damp, broken bits."

Kieren's muscles expanded. Cotton stretched, denim split. Sweat poured down his body. I took a step closer, wanting to help.

"You must see how doomed it is, baby," Bradley added. "Your sorry adolescent fling. Think for a moment. Vampire-Wolf? Vampire-Vampire? The answer is obvious."

Kieren shuffled back, awkward in his body, looked from me to his hands, then he tossed his head back, howling—still more man than animal. When he leveled his head, though, those hunter's eyes were trained on me.

"No!" Bradley exclaimed, realizing he'd lost control of the situation, my safety.

But Kieren pulled his clawed fingers into fists, ripping into himself instead, turning the inner Wolf on the outer man. His claws tore into his own flesh, cracked his bones as years ago on the railroad bridge they'd savaged mine. Blood streamed from the backs of his hands, the pierced palms, onto the midnight blue carpet. He was bleeding to protect me. Bleeding out of love for me. I'd never smelled anything so good.

I reached out for Kieren, no foreplay, no fondling, tipped him back into the nearest black leather booth, climbed him like a ladder, straddled his hips, clamped my thighs tight, and sank in. The blood—it wasn't as mild as the chicken or as overwhelming as Bradley's, but rather somewhere in between. Kieren moaned as his body went fluid, most of it anyway. Like he'd fallen under my spell. Gladly.

Kieren's blood—it was like relaxing into a pink, aromatherapy bubble bath. My muscles unwound, knots released, nether region grew effervescent. It was impossible to think, to concentrate, but I had to remember to stop. Stop drinking.

Bradley's voice floated. "Tastes divine, doesn't it? An enzyme in your saliva dissolves the clots that act to stem the flow. I stirred it into the squirrel dish, into your wine. Eventually, you'll be able to tolerate other liquids, but for now, think of blood as your mother's milk."

The table edge cut into my hip, and my right knee slipped off Kieren's thigh. *Kieren.*

"Baby, you're a smart girl. You understand. You were dead when I met you."

I bit harder, penetrated deeper. *Kieren.*

"Burying yourself in your work, holding yourself apart . . . That's what death is, separation. But you don't have to fear because of me. I'll never leave."

Shut my eyes. *Kieren.*

"That's my girl. Guzzle."

Kieren.

"So passionate, so insatiable. I won't hold you at arm's length."

Kieren.

"No need to hurry. Once he's drained, dead, we'll always be together. Neither of us will ever be alone again."

Enough. I let go, lifting my mouth from the wounds. Raised my head and licked my lips. Kieren's heart was still beating, thank God. He'd shifted back to his wholly human form as I'd drunk.

"Baby?" Bradley. He'd sounded less confident that time.

He'd keep his word, his bargain. I could hear it in his voice, feel it in my teeth.

"Quince?" Kieren whispered, his hands and throat a ragged, wet mess.

I would lose both of them, Kieren to his Wolf pack and Bradley to—what?—San Antonio. But I wouldn't give up myself or my restaurant. I wouldn't let the blood win.

I embraced my pain, pulled together my shredded humanity. My fangs retracted, my hunger cooled. "I'm here," I told Kieren, and it was true.

In the end, I'd loved him enough to let go. From afar, I would love him forever.

"*Adios.*" I told Bradley. "*Addio.*"

Good-bye.

RESTAURANTS

Sanguini's: A Very Rare Restaurant is hiring a *chef de cuisine.* Dinners only. Apply in person between 2 and 4 A.M. M–F. Ask for Quincie P. Morris, head vampire.

contorno

AUTHOR'S NOTE

In Abraham "Bram" Stoker's novel *Dracula* (1897), readers meet a hero named Quincey P. Morris, a Texan, described as "a gallant gentleman." Ultimately, Morris helps destroy Dracula by plunging a bowie knife into his heart as Jonathan Harker cuts Dracula's head off. Though Morris dies, too, Harker and his wife Mina later call their infant son "Quincey" in their late friend's honor.

Perhaps because I live in Austin, Stoker's choice of a Texan for one of the novel's heroes has long intrigued me. Though my mythology and sensibility deviate, the naming of my "Quincie P. Morris" is a tribute to one of Stoker's original vampire hunters, updated and gender flipped. Quincie became my twenty-first century hero—a young woman wrestling with an after-school job, first love, and one hell of a drinking problem.

Avid readers may also notice nods to Maurice Sendak, Mary Shelley, Joseph Sheridan Le Fanu, Nathaniel Hawthorne, Margaret Mitchell, William Shakespeare, Bob Kane, Edmond Rostand, and particularly Ovid as well as his literary/theatrical/film progeny (from "Pygmalion" to "My Fair Lady" to "Pretty Woman" to "She's All That").

Austinites will note that, within the near south and central setting, the novel adds a few streets, businesses, and residences. As tantalizing as it may seem to visit Quincie's house or swing by Sanguini's, such locales exist only within these pages.

That's it for now. Y'all take care. *Adios. Addio.* Good-bye.

ACKNOWLEDGMENTS

To Bud Smith, Niki Burnham, Austin Police
Department Public Information Officer Susan Albrecht,
and Sandy at Austin Independent School District for
answering queries and offering suggestions . . .

to Pubsters, Poddies, and YA Writers for chiming in
on even more research . . .

to Writefest 2004 and 2005 for celebrating
novel writing . . .

to Anne Bustard, Tim Crow,
Sean Petrie, and Greg Leitich Smith for thoughtful
manuscript feedback . . .

to Dianna Hutts Aston for enthusiastic matchmaking
and Ginger Knowlton for enthusiastic agenting . . .

and to Amy Ehrlich for brilliant editorial backup and
Deborah Wayshak for brilliant editing . . .

I'd like to say, *"Grazie!"*